California SHOCK

A NOVEL BY
CARLOS CHINO

Copyright © 2011 by Carlos Chino
All rights reserved

ISBN: 1-4636-3064-6
ISBN-13: 978-1-4636-3064-5
LCCN: 2011913083
CreateSpace, North Charleston, SC

To Arnell

www.carloschino.com

…and because she sent me a picture of her pussy, I felt obligated to return the favor. She wanted a picture of my "cock," her text message said. It was an evolution of dating I didn't understand, and cared little to know. But there I was, like the shirtless douchebags who take pictures of themselves in the bathroom. My pants down and my appendage out. Shame followed by guilt followed by curiosity. I took four pictures in all and sent her the one I thought most flattering. Then I waited for two minutes.

"*Oooh*," she texted back. "*Do you think you can drive up tonight and meet me in Stockton?*"

I leaned back into bed and stared at the ceiling and knew that even if I wanted to, I couldn't deny her. The girl was a physical fantasy, and although I felt like a man from a different time, it was hard to argue with the immediacy of her question. Three years ago, I might've been forced into two, maybe three awkward dates before I could feel the creases in her lips, but thanks to an impatient world, it now only took a Facebook page, a Twitter account, and a series of YouTube videos of me playing the guitar. The entire monologue of our interaction read like a script from a poorly written porno—of her poking and adding me to her friend list, of text message conversations that lasted into the night, and of bold questions compounded by bold questions, beginning with the one that, again, would've never been asked three years ago. "*How big are you?*" she had asked, and before I could reply, she had sent me a picture of her naked breasts.

We had gone from paraphrased sentences to speaking with distilled images; and after we agreed to the late-night rendezvous, I realized I had never heard the sound of her voice. I had won her with the clips of my likeness, and if that was all it would take, who was I to argue? If it makes it easier to be a man, then it must be a good thing.

"*I have to stop by a friend's house,*" I replied, "*but I should be there before one.*" She responded with a smiley face, followed by a room number to the Hilton off of March Lane. "*I'll be waiting,*" she said. So like a Prince Charming, I packed my truck and prepared for the five-hour drive from Echo Park, Los Angeles, to Northern California—to the place I have always known as the 2-0-9.

After taking a shower, I dried off and checked the e-mails on my computer, and for the hell of it, I logged onto *The Stockton Record* to see what home had been like for the last couple of years. *Forbes* magazine ranked Stockton as the most miserable city in America, citing the 8,169 foreclosures and the fact that one out of every twenty-seven households had filed for foreclosure. In response to this rat-ing, organizers held a display of civic pride, taking a group photo of two thousand people along Stockton's Miracle Mile. "Forbes doesn't get it," the quote said. "We keep the clock ticking around here. He ought to thank us. This is a celebration of the American spirit in Stockton. In fact, this event is for all the cities—Merced, Modesto, Sacramento—who made the list."

I laughed after reading the entire article, because the organizers were going to send the picture to Steve Forbes. If it were me, I would've done an updated *Godfather* and mailed the genitals of a dead horse, along with the note, "Don't fuck with us."

To paint Stockton as a vibrant, upcoming metropolis was a joke. If your city has an unemployment rate of 17.6 percent and ranks second in California violent crimes, you should be doing more. For some reason, I blame Facebook. A picture doesn't solve problems. But then again, I had a hand in all those foreclosures, and I had nothing but a savings account of a weaker dollar to show for it.

The police blotter caught my eye, so I clicked on the article and read the lines that felt like the Stockton I remembered.

A twenty-three-year-old man was stabbed by three men after talking to a woman and yelling racial slurs.

A sixteen-year-old girl was struck in the back of the neck with a cricket bat.

Three boys rang the front doorbell of a vacant house, then went into the backyard and stole a bicycle.

Police responded to a 911 call after a woman said that some youths came to her door and tried to beat up her husband.

A thirty-year-old man was arrested on misdemeanor vandalism after a knife fight with his wife.

A fifteen-year-old boy was sent to the hospital after being tied to and dragged behind a vehicle full of teenagers.

A suspicious box was reported in front of a building on the 2200 block of San Joaquin.

A church official called to report he found a statue of death, a skull, a bullet, and some other items in a bush outside St. Luke's Catholic Church.

I opened my bedroom door after grabbing my acoustic guitar and took three steps before being stopped by two of my roommates, Darvin and Hutch. They were like me, caught in the fading tide of their twenties, but trying desperately to hold on, unable to grasp that no matter how hard we tried, we were on the other side of hip. Both of them were working IT jobs they had no passion for, while I remained jobless, living off of a combination of unemployment checks from the telemarketing job and the savings account from my previous life as a loan officer. "Vegas," the two of them said, as if to conjure the memories of college road trips. "We're going to Vegas."

"Not tonight," I declined. "It's only Wednesday."

They stepped aside to let me through but followed me to the kitchen, watching me and waiting for a change of heart, like all the other times in college when I spent money because it wasn't tomorrow's money—the adult money we'd have to save and never spend. "Hutch met a girl on Craigslist," explained Darvin. "And this time, it's legit."

I took a bottle of water from the refrigerator and began to drink. "Legit?" I asked. "And by that, do you mean a legit girl who wants to hang out, or do you mean legit, as in the other kind?"

"It's Craigslist," said Hutch, pausing to let the idea run through the air. "She's out of our league, but it'll only cost a couple hundred."

"And get this," added Darvin. "She said if he gets two of his friends to come, she'll invite two of her friends, meaning we could theoretically be with all three of them for only the price of one."

"Ask someone else," I said. "I hate paying for sex."

"Come on, Cali," they begged, their words coming slow and from deep within an urgency that told me I was their last resort. They've already asked the other guys, I thought, thinking of Jason and Will in the bedroom upstairs. And since those two were broke and unemployed, Darvin and Hutch were asking me, hoping I'd break the bank on my savings and make the evening an even better night. "That's okay," I replied. "I'll pass."

"If it's because of the money," said Hutch, "just think of it in terms of cutting through the bullshit."

"Yeah," explained Darvin. "You pay no matter what. Whether it's through dinner and five dates, or whether it's an ad on the Internet. Only this time, you don't have to waste a week to get that first kiss."

I shook my head and closed the refrigerator, taking the bottle along with my guitar. "We've had this argument before," I said. "You make perfect sense, but I enjoy the buildup and the chase." They walked with me through the side door and into the driveway, where my truck awaited me. "Besides," I continued, "I have to head over to Redondo Beach for a quick gig, and then I'm off to Stockton."

"Stockton?" they asked.

"I'm meeting a girl tonight," I said. "And on top of that, I should visit my parents. I haven't seen them since I was released from the Honor Farm."

"But it's been years since you've been in prison," shrugged Hutch.

"Exactly," I said. "It's overdue."

They stood on the stoop, wide-mouthed and still hoping, but I took the keys from my pocket and started the ignition, dropping the gear into drive, the backdrop of the rustic house painting a scene of five men who graduated from college, the bond of attending the same university and immigrant Filipino ancestry the only reason for the sustained friendship. "I'll be back in two days," I said, and pulled away from the organized fraternity house we called home, taking the side streets to the highways and heading on a southwest course to the expensive beach house of a dying woman who had recently become a dying friend.

The drive was less than thirty minutes, not enough time for reflection or creative thoughts, so I rolled my window down and let the sunset sweep through the cabin of my truck, watching the line of airplanes build across the 405 as they waited their turn to land at LAX. I wondered where they were coming from. What stories and what kind of adventures did the passengers have pocketed in their suitcases? I'd always wanted to travel, but somewhere between my teenage years and the milieu of my early twenties, I had grown to fear flying and the thought of crashing in a ball of engine-fueled fire. The nightmare had existed long before the events of 9/11 and intensified in the years following.

"Come inside," said the husband, and welcomed me into the mansion, offering, as usual, a glass of pale ale to set the evening at ease. "Miranda's asleep and holding on," he continued. I accepted the beer and carried it with me along with my guitar, walking through the series of opulent hallways and into the bedroom that opened into a perfect view of the Pacific Ocean. The combination of rippled water and dusk ascended into the house.

"Miranda," I whispered, and took my usual seat away from the bed and in the far corner where I would be heard and not seen. "I missed you," I said. "Did you miss me?"

The only response she gave was silence followed by the beep of the machines that were connected to her veins. It had only been a week, but I could tell things were getting worse. She appeared more tired, and her cheeks had somehow risen out of her skin. Was she asleep? Or in a coma? I couldn't tell, but from the look of things, I knew that this would either be the last performance or the second to last performance I'd have with her. It was a thought I'd step away from in order to appreciate, and after taking that moment, I adjusted the guitar in my lap and prepared to play the Brazilian song she had come to love as her favorite sound to hear before falling asleep.

Miranda first met me at a coffeehouse in Hollywood, and because she didn't like the music I was playing, she asked if I could play anything else. "Something Spanish," she said, and I told her I'd play a Brazilian song I learned from a friend.

"Okay, cool guy," she said, dropping a dollar into my guitar case. "Play it."

"On one condition," I nodded.

"And what would that be?"

I pointed to the CDs sitting next to me. "Buy one."

"But I already told you," she replied, "I think you're talented, but I'm not a fan of that type of music."

We would eventually agree on the compromise that she'd buy the CD if she liked what I played, and after I proved myself, she handed me the ten-dollar bill from her purse. "I'll probably just give it to my younger brother," she said. "The young ones love this stuff, but I don't think they've ever heard it from an acoustic guitar before."

"That's part of my charm," I told her with a smile.

Miranda laughed and asked for my number, saying she'd like to hire me for personal performances. At first I refused, because I saw myself as a serious musician and not a one-man mariachi band, but then she told me she was sick. "It's the kind of sick you don't come back from," she confessed, "and yes, if you're feeling guilty, it's because I want you to feel guilty. My dying wish is to hear the waves breaking outside of my house and the sound of music in the background."

She wasn't much older than me, and by that I mean she had more to live than what she was given. I watched her now, in her bed, the time and years being sucked from her body, the cap on her head covering the bald spots from her treatment. A mother and wife reduced to an end-of-days. Miranda was unrecognizable if not for the eyes that showed even when closed. "I'm going to play now," I told her. "I tried learning some new stuff, but I'll start with the song you like."

My fingers stretched and relaxed into place. I took a breath and watched her for a final time before closing my eyes to imagine a healthy Miranda and what she must've been like before I knew her, the song beginning with the entrance of slow strums that mirrored the walk through an adobe-tiled trail.

I strummed the way my piano teachers always told me to play music, attempting to find the hidden notes between the measures, pressing and plucking the strings so she could take the melody with her to the ever-after. When I was done with the song, I played it again to make sure; and when that was done, I played it again, repeating the song on an endless loop, and only after twelve rounds and being interrupted by a visitor did I stop to let my hands rest. I felt in tune with the heat from her body and would have cried, but we were no longer alone.

The visitor bowed his head to apologize for the intrusion, and I smiled and bowed in return. He looked like an old friend, possibly someone she knew from childhood, because he walked with a familiar intimacy of the house. "Is she asleep?" he asked, unbuttoning his gray suit and sitting in the old recliner next to the bed.

I nodded yes and stared at the way he combed the bangs from his eyes. It was an expensive suit combined with an expensive haircut. Whatever elitist club Miranda and her family were in, he too would also be a member, if not the vice president. The man carried himself with just the right amount of arrogance and humility, and as he watched Miranda sleep, he put his hands over hers in a farewell embrace.

I thought of rich characters from famous novels and the dinner parties they must've had and the articulate way they must've used their words. The Gatsby's. The philosophies of Ayn Rand. The artists from a Hemingway plot. He nudged himself close to Miranda, and just when I was about to stand and leave, he cradled her neck and covered his mouth against her ear, like telling her a dark secret, whispering words that sounded like the wind.

Should I leave, I asked myself. I didn't want to ruin his moment, so I closed my eyes again, and played softly, a new song I had been working on since the time she first hired me, trying my best to retain the ambiance, dancing my fingers against the strings and grazing them in tune with the somber mood.

The man whispered for a long while, and when he was done, I could hear him sigh against the back of the recliner. "It makes you wonder," he said, speaking equally to himself and to the stranger across the room. "What is it all worth?" he asked. "What is it all worth," he said again.

I stopped playing, and this time I watched him lean forward, setting his elbows against his knees and clasping his hands in a prayer. "Are you the musician?" he asked, breaking his silence after a few minutes. "They told me about you and said you were very good." I didn't know what to say, so I said nothing. "I live in Pennsylvania," he continued, "and I've known she's been sick, but I could never bring myself to visit until now." He raised his eyes to meet mine. "I'm a terrible friend," he confessed. "I've never done well with death; in fact, I avoid it at all costs."

It was dark in the room, except for the lamp next to the bed, and I continued my silence and allowed him to vent his frustrations. He nodded his head, clicking his tongue against his teeth, turning to see Miranda. Waiting. Thinking. Tapping his shoes against the carpet. Then nothingness.

"Do you know anything?" he asked.

"I don't know anything about your relationship with Miranda," I said. "I can only speak for the short time I've known her, and what I know is a woman who enjoyed driving down to Oceanside and parking her car off of Wisconsin Avenue because she liked listening to the way the rocks bubbled as the waves rolled over them. That's all we ever did together, and every time we did, she'd make me play the same song over and over again, and I'd watch her bundled in her sweater, hoping she'd fall asleep."

"Do you know the name of the song?" he asked.

"No."

"Were you playing it before I came in?"

"Yes," I replied.

He reached under the recliner and opened a secret compartment, pulling a bottle of Scotch and a glass. "We grew up in this room," he said, smiling, and poured a shot. "Would you mind playing that song for me?"

"No," I said, and cleared my throat, putting my hands into the familiar position.

It's beautiful, he would later say, before sipping four shots and falling asleep next to his friend; and I continued to play, because if anything, I knew I owed her this moment, the amazing thing being the tingle I felt inside, knowing that while I strummed to give her a piece of music, she slept and gave me something back, a feeling I could hold with me whenever I performed, the feeling my piano teachers always told me to play with. Soul.

When I was finished, I stood up to leave, and as I stepped toward the door, the man in the gray suit rose to his feet and met me. "So do you play locally?" he asked, shaking my hand.

"Kind of; sort of," I said.

"Are you in a band, or do you mostly play solo?"

I let go of his palm and told him I was Cali Shock, a son of a hippy nobody, and, like every other dreamer that moves to LA, hoping for the one chance to make it big. And then he asked me if I had a CD to sell.

"I do," I replied, "but you wouldn't like my music."

"If it's anything like what you've played tonight, I can't see how I wouldn't."

"That's just it," I sighed. "I don't normally play that kind of stuff. Otherwise I'd be like every other cat with an acoustic, singing with a crooning hitch and a raspy backwash."

"Then what do you play?" he asked.

"Rap," I said.

"Rap?" he asked.

"Folk-rap," I told him with a smile.

The man sucked his lower lip and laughed quietly. "Then I definitely need to buy it," he said.

We each took turns to say good-bye to Miranda, and when it was my turn to be alone with her, I knelt at her bedside and tried to squeeze the last of my tears, but there was nothing. The good-bye was something we had been saying to each other since we first said hello; and for her sake, I held her hand and prayed for the final end.

Something inside me said that this would be the last time I'd see her alive, but in the depths of that moment, there was nothing remarkable. The Miranda I had known had already died, and these last bits that slept in front of me were leftovers of someone else.

I kissed Miranda for the second time in my life and walked out of the room.

The husband was sipping coffee in the kitchen. He stopped me to say his usual farewell, handing me an envelope of money and chatting about the prognosis of his wife. We all spoke with reverence, and I promised to play again the following week, but by the way he was talking, he confirmed my suspicions.

"We're going to increase the morphine," he said. "It's only a matter of time."

The man in the gray suit followed me to my truck, and after digging behind the driver seat for one of the twenty copies I had left, I handed him my CD and told him it was ten dollars.

"Ten dollars?" he asked. "Is that all?" I shrugged and he handed me a hundred-dollar bill because he didn't have any change. "It's okay," the man said. "It's for the CD and the time with Miranda."

I nodded a thank you, and he told me if it was any good, he'd refer me to a friend who could help me with my music.

"It's okay," I explained. "I've got a manager and we've got some things in the works."

He tapped the CD case against his free hand and watched me get into my truck. "And what kind of works do you have going?" he asked. "If you don't mind me prying."

"I don't know," I said, turning the ignition. "If he's really a man of his word, then I should expect a call any day from now, saying I've got a record deal and a nice little signing bonus."

"So do you trust him?"

"I've got to," I said, shaking his hand. "I've got nowhere else to go."

He patted the side door as I drove away, and I gave him a look and a wave from my rearview mirror, taking the road through the Pacific Highway and back east to Artesia, before heading north on the 405—where my melancholy thoughts regressed, giving way to my sexual fantasies. The woman in the Hilton, I told myself. She'll be waiting on the bed no matter what time I arrive. I knew this as fact because I'd been trained in the *Boiler Room* philosophy of hunting. To ABC. Always Be Closing. The ethos imbedded in my mind whenever I spoke to a woman. And because of the way she took her pictures, I knew I had closed her. I knew that she'd be waiting for me, even if it meant waiting until tomorrow.

I knew this from experience. Because no matter what I did to bury my past, whether it be playing guitar for the sick, or chasing my dreams as a musician, deep down I knew who I was.

I was a pawn in the chess game that swindled the world.

When you grow up, no one ever tells you how the truths become lies and how the good becomes bad, and the bad becomes good. The secret is that you figure it out as you go, but when you do, the meaning of life smears itself into an abstract you can never understand.

Jay Warner found me in a dive bar near Sacramento and sold me on the idea of becoming rich. I had just graduated from UCLA with a degree in Computer Engineering. I had no prospects for employment because of my insufferable grades and was inclined to work retail at a shopping mall, but after meeting Jay through a series of mutual friends, he convinced me to take a job in his Stockton branch.

He was only a year older than me, and although he never attended college, I could tell he had been schooled in the art of making money. "I've got a condo in San Francisco," he said, "a house in Sacramento, and a bevy of sports cars and one-night stands. If you want proof," he continued, "look at my watch, and count the five thousand dollars rolled in my wallet."

Jay Warner spoke fast and with an unflinching confidence. He said he had no choice because he was plain and overweight, but by the way he spoke, you could never tell.

"Watch the movie *Boiler Room*," he said, after taking me on a tour of his Stockton branch. "And when you do, remember: no one ever cares what you do; they only care if you make money."

The movie starred Giovanni Ribisi, Vin Diesel, Nia Long, and Nicky Katt; it was an ode to the greed from the movie *Wall Street*. A make-your-money-quick-and-be-prepared-for-the-fallout kind of film that revealed many truths. That I would make some quick money. That I would sleep with hookers and snort cocaine. And that we would all eventually be caught.

It was an embrace of the good and an ignorance of the bad when I signed the papers and became a loan officer for Jay Warner. He liked me from the start and promised to get me deeper into his schemes if I proved I was an earner. Being a loan officer was step one, and entering his inner circle would be the end game. It would be there that I would learn how to steal the real money.

The devil is the devil, but in a competitive job market, you take the job he gives you. You develop blinders on your peripheral and forget about the people you're screwing with and the future you're destroying, because happiness means nothing if you don't have anything to show for it.

I proved myself to Jay by selling greed to people who couldn't afford the gamble. I'd drive to the office in the morning and work the phones, helping to refinance their mortgages because it seemed like a win-win for everybody. The customer would get cash back and a lower monthly rate, and we would make our cut, charging a percentage based on the size of the loan, splitting the pot to 60/40, with Jay getting the bigger share.

It was more money than I'd ever made delivering pizzas in college, and I liked the fact that the harder I worked, the more money I could make. But it was a drying well I should've had the foresight to see; and instead of paying attention to the signs, I got caught up like the rest of the loan officers. We were college kids playing pretend, ill-equipped and naïve to the excesses of our profits. The weekends in hotels. The night clubs in San Francisco. The booze. The drugs. The sex.

It didn't matter to Jay, because he was making it big, taking his cut from his three branches in Sacramento, Stockton, and Modesto, walking away with a yearly salary every month. And if it weren't for my arrest, I would've been there for the bigger money, and I would've been there for the harder fall, but it was a blessing in disguise when they arrested me.

I was in jail with a sizable savings account, and had it not been for the lifestyle I snorted into my nose, I would've had more.

The world caught up with the subprime mortgages while I served the term of my sentence; and America lost their jobs and their homes as Jay Warner fled the country with a myriad of charges—all of them having to do with money laundering from his one-hundred-million dollar Ponzi scheme.

By the time I reached the Grapevine, my car was running on empty, so I exited the highway and filled my gas tank at the 76 station where Southern California meets Central California. It was a little after ten, and if I sped through the drive from Bakersfield to Stockton, I would've arrived on time. "*Where are you?*" she kept asking me.

"*I'm three hours away*," I replied.

"*Hurry Cali! I'm getting sleepy.*"

The girl was demanding. If she were my girlfriend, I would've called and told her to go to sleep. Women want everything, and no matter how hard they try to mask it, their true colors will betray them. I hardly knew her, but I knew enough to know she wanted a piece of my dream. That if in fact I did make it in the music industry, she would be right beside me to enjoy the spoils. It's the brush of the Internet. If you put it online, then it automatically adds value to your life. I was just as guilty as she was, but instead of trying to make it in Hollywood, she was in search of as many confirmations as possible that, yes, she was beautiful. Make her friend list bigger and comment on all of her sexy pictures. That's all she ever wanted.

I turned my phone off after filling my truck. As I drove north, I touched the buttons on my CD player and listened to the music I recorded from the twenty-thousand-dollar-studio I built in my bedroom. Am I any good, I wondered. Is there a future in folk-rap? Or am I just kidding myself?

My *Resin Hits* demo contained fifteen tracks; and somewhere, saved in my computer, I had a hundred more waiting to be edited and refined. I drove and critiqued my music, searching for a reason to retreat and surrender, but much like the fantasy girl waiting for me in Stockton, I had too many hits on my website to turn back. I was on the cusp of being famous, and the thought never strayed far from my mind. It scared me.

I thought about calming myself with a phone call to my best friend from high school, Luke Walker, but ever since he lost his house, he stopped answering my phone calls. I'd have to finish the drive to Stockton alone with my guilt; and for those three hours, it was all I could think about.

The two police officers entered the Stockton branch with a warrant for the breaking-and-entering charge that had occurred two weeks prior. I hadn't told anyone what happened and excused my work absences on a flu that I had been battling, so it was a surprise to everyone when they saw the police waiting in the lobby. I was railing lines of cocaine from the table in the conference room, doing business as usual, getting high with the other loan officers while farting into the PA system. Had I known they'd be back to arrest me, I would've closed the loan waiting on my desk and I would've dropped the ecstasy pill hidden inside my filing cabinet.

They cuffed me, and I was booked and fingerprinted at the county jail like before, only this time, instead of locking me in Intake 3 with a roommate, I was processed and sent to Intake 4 with my own room.

The incident in question happened on a Saturday night while I was partying at a house in the Brookside development of Stockton. I was cross-faded on a mixture of Jack Daniels, marijuana, and cocaine, and for some reason, I left the house in search of a liquor store so I could buy a pack of Parliament Lights to smoke and cap the success of a day that saw me close my biggest loan.

I never found a place to buy my cigarettes, and upon returning to the house, I had gotten lost and tried opening the door to the wrong address. I knocked on the door and peered through the windows and figured my co-workers were playing another prank on me. "Open up," I ordered them, but when I received no reply, I took matters into my own hands and took a decorative gnome from the front yard and threw it into the living room window, which shattered, allowing me to crawl through.

The house was dark, and I was too drunk to notice it was empty. "I'm hungry," I whispered, taking a nap on the bed in the master bedroom, which in turn must've set off their piece-of-shit alarm system that should've gone off when I destroyed their window. "Fuck," I cursed, and struggled back through the hallways and into the kitchen, where I grabbed a case of beer.

It was the only thing I took from the place, and when I opened the front door and staggered to the streets, the off-duty police officer next door tackled me and held me down until the proper authorities arrived. I was arrested and spent all of Sunday and Monday in Intake 3 with my cellie, a white guy booked on an assault-and-battery charge. He gave me the mattress on the floor next to the bed, and could tell I was suffering from the post-trauma of being stripped naked and changed into my new orange jumpsuit. "It isn't so bad," he would later tell me. "The officers must've looked at you and taken you for a white guy. And if it pays to be anything in this joint, it pays to be a white guy." I didn't have the energy to explain the mixture of Caucasian and Filipino blood in my veins, and went along with the code the prisoners had come to govern themselves with.

The caste system was separated into Whites, Blacks, Mexicans, and the Others. The Others were a mixture of Asian, Arabian, and anyone else who didn't fit into a group. My cellie deduced that I was categorized as a White because they never mixed races in a cell. "We're first in line, and we never associate or take food from anyone else," he said. "Remember that."

I expected to get raped, but my fears were assuaged, and he guided me through the routine. If I wanted to take a shower, I would have to wait my turn. The prisoners would never allow more than one person in the shower, because of all the things to hate, they hated faggots and gays. He told me they'd send any faggot back to the guards, where they would take the faggot to another Intake.

For two days during the initial arrest, I waited for my court date with the judge. I woke up in the morning and ate my breakfast, taking fifteen minutes to down the oatmeal, the grits, the eggs, the mystery meat, and my orange juice and milk.

The lunch and dinner took place at eleven and six o'clock, and we were allowed only an hour of recreation time, which was wasted in front of the television instead of by the phone, where I could call my parents or even a lawyer. My rationale for contacting neither was based on the hatred of my parents and the insistence on keeping my money. If I hired an expensive lawyer, I might've gotten out sooner, but I'd probably be broke. This was clearly a misunderstanding, and I trusted the court system to sift through the rubble and see it. After all, this was only my first offense. What kind of sentence could they give a first-timer on a nonviolent crime?

My prospects looked good during my arraignment. The judge gave me a "no complaint" and I was taken back to booking and immediately released. Only when I was arrested that second time at the Stockton branch did I realize the seriousness I had gotten myself into. The public defender assigned to my case explained the situation, that I was facing a felony charge of second degree burglary.

"But this is my first offense," I told him. "If I really wanted to steal anything, I wouldn't have stolen a case of beer."

The public defender understood where I was coming from, but he told me the family whose house I broke into was a close friend of the district attorney. "He's going to make an example out of you," he said. "I tried to make a deal, but the only thing I can get is a misdemeanor vandalism charge with a sentencing of one year at the Honor Farm."

I eventually broke down and called my parents, and convinced them to post bail, allowing me to tie the loose ends from work, giving me a month to close as many accounts as I could—which was the only thing that mattered to Jay, who didn't care that I was a dead man walking. "I have a couple good-bye presents waiting for you," he said on my last day of work, and handed me a key to a hotel room in the Hilton off of March Lane. "Consider it your severance package before you enter the clink."

I faced the judge three times after my second arrest. The first time I pled "Not guilty"; the second time, the lawyers weighed the evidence against me; and the third time, I was sentenced to the shitty deal my public defender brokered.

He explained the details to me and said I would only have to serve four to six months of my sentencing. After that, I'd be free and could finally put the incident in the past.

My parents drove me to the Honor Farm, and as we said our good-byes, I stepped away and looked at the two of them. I was grateful they had bailed me out, but when I observed their faces, I could only feel the embarrassment I had felt throughout my youth. My hippy father was white, the kind of nerdy loser whose inept social skills would hinder any romantic relationship. He wore thick, framed glasses because he needed to, and he always wore black.

He found my mother in a Filipino catalog and first met her at a whorehouse, near the Natividad province of Pampanga that she was named after. My mom led a destitute life, and because of it, she could never understand anything except the color of money. They were an odd couple, without a doubt; and whenever I looked at them, I could only see them for what they were. My father was an agent for an insurance company, and my mother worked with the other mail-order brides as a manager at the McDonald's off of Kettleman and Highway 99.

"Tell my sister I'll do my best to be there when she graduates from high school," I said, and turned toward the Honor Farm.

When my radio picked up the KWIN station 98.3, I knew I had returned home. The 2-0-9 is an area code that reaches as far south as Merced and as far north as Galt, but if you wanted to get technical, the 2-0-9 is an attitude that encompasses Modesto, Stockton, Lodi, and Tracy; and although I had left the attitude in my past, I could never forget it.

I grew up in North Stockton, close to Fox Creek, which was where I learned how to take a punch—and, more importantly, where I learned how to throw one back. As I drove through the final leg of my homecoming, I stared at my knuckles. The scar close to my ring finger was from a fight when I was twelve. I punched the guy so hard it cracked my hand, but my opponent, a fourteen-year-old from Kelley Drive, kicked me in the stomach, rupturing my appendix and sending me to the hospital.

I pulled my vanity mirror down to assess the age behind my eyes, and when I found nothing, I flipped the mirror back and exited March Lane, pulling into the parking lot beside the Hilton at a quarter after one. "I'm late," I whispered, and walked to the hotel, carrying only my guitar.

I was exhausted, and my legs were numb from sitting, so I tried to breathe the fresh air outside of my truck, attempting to revive the mood. The woman inside the room would be beautiful, and because I had never kissed anyone I had never spoken to, I didn't know how to start. Should I knock and take hold of her, I thought. Should I call her first and tell her I'm here? Or should I text her and continue the cycle?

None of that would matter once we were engulfed in each other's embrace, and I imagined how that would feel as I entered the lobby and proceeded to the elevator. Her text message said she was in room 228, and I followed the directions from the wall. The hallways were quiet with expectation and before I could turn the corner for her room, the door from 202 opened, and out popped a young woman with dirty blonde hair.

She had the eyes of a woman in her forties and the face of a twenty-year-old. "Oh," she said, with a wispy voice. "I thought you were my friend."

I nodded my head and continued to walk, but the woman from 202 followed behind me. "You any good?" she asked, staring at my guitar. "Cuz I'd love to listen if you got the time."

I stopped to examine her face, checking to see if she was high. Her eyes were red, but that could've been from sleeping or from drinking. "It's kind of late," I said. "Maybe next time."

"But there won't be a next time," she replied. "Haven't you heard? Tomorrow's never guaranteed."

"I agree," I nodded, "but I've got my own friend down the hall, and she's been waiting for me all night."

The woman lifted her eyebrows and gave me a puppy-dog look. She extended her hand to shake mine and told me her name was Tate. "And it's my birthday," she said. "You can't leave me so unsatisfied."

The ploys of attractive women, I thought. "You can't go through life like this," I laughed. "You're going to use your pretty smile and get what you want. What happens when your smile ain't so pretty anymore?" Her puppy-look transformed into a smirk. "Save your begging for a boy who actually wants you." But my words did little to deter her, and she positioned herself in front of me, blocking my way to room 228.

"Okay," I gave in. "If you can prove it's your birthday, I'll play a song for you."

Tate led me back to her room in 202, and as soon as I entered, I was greeted by a group of six women who were positioned in a half-circle against an empty corner. I counted three couples of lesbians in all, and I knew they were lesbian because each one had the short haircut of a young boy from England, with the bangs hanging perfectly coiffed to the side. "Hey guys," Tate said. "Look what I found. I found a boy with a guitar."

"Hey, boy-with-a-guitar," replied one of the lesbians.

I was startled, but not because they were lesbians. I had seen many things in Hollywood, and because of my miniature success, I was immune to most things considered counter-culture. My surprise, however, stemmed from the late hour of the night and the fact that I thought she'd be alone. "Girls," continued Tate, "this is…" She stopped and tilted her head. "I'm so sorry. I never got your name."

"My name is Cali," I said. "Cali Shock."

"Cali?" she asked. "Is that short for something else?"

I took a seat in the half-circle and told them my mother's name was Natividad, after the village she was born in, and that when she had me in America, she wanted to continue the tradition and named me after California. "My full name," I said, "is California Dizon Shock, and my sister, because she was born in San Ramon, is Ramona Dizon Shock."

The girls watched me as I spoke and they nodded slowly. It was the same thing I had seen in Tate, and when I spotted the plate of cookies next to one of the lesbians, I realized why. It didn't smell like the skunk of marijuana because they had baked it into the cookies, and instead of glasses of alcohol, each one had a glass of milk. The fat burly one with sideburns that seemed to reach her chin saw me eyeing the batch and offered me a bite, but I declined.

"Dizon?" asked another one. "Is that your mother's maiden name?" She had an exotic smile that complemented her reddish-brown hair.

"Yes."

"Are you Filipino?" she asked.

"Yes." I said again. "How did you know?"

"Because my middle name is Bustos, which is also my mother's maiden name." She smiled and leaned back into the wall. "I'm half-Filipino, half-German," she continued. "You wouldn't also happen to be a military brat by any chance?"

"No," I replied. "I'm the rare but often joked about product of the mail-order bride."

She laughed and said it wasn't so bad if my parents were still together, and after we reminisced about the circumstances of our blood, Tate interrupted, saying enough was enough. She wanted me to play music. "I didn't ask you to talk," Tate added, and showed me her driver's license. "See?" she said as she pointed at it. "Today is my birthday."

I crossed my legs Indian style and set the guitar on my lap, tuning the strings and watching the anticipating faces. They were high, and I thought about playing a rhyme I wrote inspired by the novel *1984*, but I figured it would go over their heads and they'd only enjoy the beat. Ignorance is bliss, I said to myself. So then I thought about playing an upbeat song, something fun and less serious. Their eyes half-closed and minutes from unconsciousness, I changed my mind and decided to play an AA Bondy cover I learned after meeting him at a music festival in Seattle.

There was the original way to perform the tune, and then there was the upbeat rendition I'd used in my own sessions, where I fused my own lyrics within Bondy's melody. I could've gone either way, but I was bored and chose to riff the song, using the original verse and melody as a bass line to keep me in rhythm. It was a testament of how far I'd developed as an artist and a songwriter; of how no matter where I stood in the music canon, I'd consider myself an accomplished musician regardless.

"This song is called *Killed myself when I was young*," I said. "It's by an artist from Alabama."

I watched their crooked lips, disoriented from the THC, and began by dancing the bass with a tap on the wooden frame of my acoustic, intensifying the speed into a comfortable pace before invoking the words:

> *Killed myself when I was young*
> *With my fingers on a poison gun*
> *With my fingers on a poison gun*
> *'Cause I had to come back new*
> *'Cause I had to come back new*
> *Wanna walk on the ocean blue*
> *Wanna walk on the ocean blue*
>
> *And I'm gonna leave this town*
> *And I'm gonna leave this town*

With the people all tumbling down
With the people all tumbling down
And my boots on the diamond road
And my boots on the diamond road
Behind such a heavy load
Behind such a heavy load

And I will come back someday
If I do not lose my way
If I do not lose my way
Don't weep, my girl so true
Don't weep, my girl so true
Let the train whistle cry for you
Let the train whistle cry for you

The original plays for just under four minutes, and I riffed the song for fifteen, ending with applause from the lesbians, who, from their initial reaction, I could tell were surprised. They must've thought I was a ballad singer, and while I do believe in a place and time for soulful love songs, I'd rather make an audience move. It was enough for a requested encore, but I said no. Leave them wanting more, is the saying the old-timers taught me, so I bowed and said good-bye.

Tate led me to the door, and for a second I thought we could kiss, but her boyfriend opened the door as I was departing. He said his name, but I never cared to remember. He looked like a man without a spine, like someone who hid behind e-mails and memos. "He plays music too," Tate said, and I imagined him as a pianist who couldn't play Chopin. I was a struggling musician, and nothing bothered me more than a poser.

People think a voice constitutes music. They think a memorized piano solo requires thought. They believe image sells records and records need image. But whatever happened to playing? Of talking and letting the notes hang from our mouths. Feeding a hunger until there just ain't no more.

I let the boyfriend take his girlfriend back to the bedroom of lesbians, and I slung my guitar over my shoulder and walked to room 228. It was a little after two o'clock, so I knocked hard to get her attention. This didn't work at first, but I persisted, and after the fourth time, I finally received my answer. "Who is it?" a voice asked.

"It's me, Cali."

She opened the door, wearing lingerie that would never wrinkle if she tried.

And if I were a truly lost soul. If my life were in shambles. If I didn't believe in myself. If I believed in hugs instead of kisses. If I had never learned to touch a woman. If I would've listened to the after-school specials. To "Just Say No."

Then maybe I would've grabbed her reluctantly and made love while holding back. Then maybe I would've let her feel sorry for me. The hero who doesn't want to be. The sad clown. The morose.

"Hey," she said.

"Hey," I replied, and stepped inside, dropping my guitar on the floor and pushing her back to the bed. I have none of those feelings, I told myself, and then I kissed her lips like a fantasy and pulled her hair like a man.

☙❦❧

At some point in a man's life, staring into the mirror means looking at the wrinkles and searching for the scars. I cupped my hands to the running water from the sink and splashed a dab into my eyes. No matter how hard I tried to forget, my past was etched onto my body. I stared at myself, at the way I had changed since leaving Stockton, and I wondered about nothing—the recurring theme of my life.

The fantasy girl was asleep on the bed, and I rejoined her moments later, taking a spot on the left side of the mattress, the two of us still naked. It was my favorite part of having sex. The hour or so later when it's just you and her, lying together but alone. She smelled of lotion, and as we cuddled, it was silent, the part I'd always missed.

Her head rested on my chest and my arm held her close, with only the wind ticking against the plastic curtains for a soundtrack. I could stay here forever, I wanted to say, but if I told her that, she would've thought the comment pertained to her. The reality was that it could've been most any woman and I would've been happy.

She was someone to hold, and that's all I ever wanted—someone to hold.

※

My telephone vibrated against the nightstand, and I nudged the fantasy woman away from me, sitting up with the bed sheet wrapped around my waist. "Hello," I said.

It was my manager on the other end, and by the way he was talking, I could tell it had been a long night, and that there would be some news worth listening to. "You'll never guess what," he said, "but I was up in Malibu, partying with a certain record label."

"Enough with the preamble," I told him. "Just tell me if it's good news."

"I sold them, Cali. You are and will be the rapping reincarnation of Bob Dylan." He took a breath. "I sunk my teeth, and told them you'd be to folk-rap what the Beatles were to rock. I told them you could transcend genres. That you could usher the revolution."

He was on a roll, but like every meeting we'd ever had, I had to stop him and ask. "But what about my age?" I said. "And what about my look?"

"It doesn't matter, Cali. Your age and your look are the foundation for what you've been creating, and that's what I told them. You're Asian, but you're also white. You're older, but you're at an age when the music becomes less pop and more refined. It's perfect for what they've been looking for, and that's what I sold them on." I stood up with the bed sheet and walked to the balcony of the hotel room. "You're the American Dream," he continued. "You are the son of America and America is ready to see you."

"So what now?" I asked him.

"So what now," he replied back. "Cali, we've come a long way since signing together, and I promised you the world, and now the world is knocking on your door."

I pulled the phone away from my ear to look at the bullshit he was shoveling into it, and then I asked him to speak English. "Don't sell me," I said. "Just tell me the truth. What is the truth?" I asked.

He paused and agreed to calm down. "The truth is that I've got a meeting with them on Friday. They want to hear you, and they want to see a compilation of all your performances."

"And then what?"

"And then it happens, buddy. And then it happens." I could hear the saliva dripping from his lips. "We create the market for folk-rap. Then from folk-rap to folk. From folk to rock. And on and on until you've saturated and explored every genre of music. We sell you on the premise of not one record," he went on, "but on the promise of many, with all the concerts and sales that go with it."

I stretched my neck back and stared at the sky while he detailed our final moves. If the meeting went well, there'd either be another meeting for a sit-down, or they'd sign me right there. "Good job," I told him.

The sky was changing from the blackness I had become used to and into the morning it had always become. I dragged the bed sheet inside the hotel and crawled on top of the woman, kissing her neck and pulling her hair so she could congratulate my success. We had neither the time nor the energy for bedroom conversation, and ended the relationship the way it began: with a passionate but informal touch that would never quench what we were thirsty for.

"I want you," I lied.

"I want you too," she whispered back.

⁂

The Honor Farm consists of three levels, and in the six months I served, I graduated through all three, making friends with a forty-five-year-old white guy they called "Lefty," who got the nickname because someone caught him masturbating at summer camp when he was twelve. "I'm really right-handed," he explained, "but they called me Lefty cuz it sounded better." He was serving a year for a DUI, driving under the influence, and because he was older than most of us and had been through the system, the shot-callers would lean on him. On one occasion, during my stay in the first level of the Honor Farm known as The Ghetto, I caught a crazy old-timer stealing my Oreo cookies from under my bunk.

The Ghetto looks like an army barracks with sixty beds sprawled across in rows, and because we were in such close proximity of each other, there was an understood code among the inmates. In layman's terms, that meant keeping your hands and your dick to yourself.

"Did ya steal this man's Oreo cookies?" asked Lefty when he approached the old-timer.

We surrounded the old man's bunk with eight inmates, and in spite of the odds, the old-timer stuck to his guns and refused to surrender. "No," he croaked, smoking a cigarette. "I ain't stolen shit from nobody."

Lefty put his forearm against the top bunk and watched the old man who sat motionless on the bottom. It was quiet for a few minutes, and then Lefty grabbed the man's bag and searched for my Oreos, which he found near the bottom, in a zippered compartment beside a small stash of weed. "Are these yours?" he asked me.

I nodded.

"You got any explanation for this?" asked Lefty of the old-timer.

But the old man said nothing.

We all looked at each other and waited for something to happen. Are we going to kill this guy, I thought. Are we *really* going to kill him over a sleeve of Oreos? I felt ashamed for the old guy, but I was caught in the mob mentality. Fuck him, I said to myself. If he can't man-up and confess, I'll do whatever Lefty tells me.

The inmates waited for the signal, and before it was given, Lefty surveyed the group and cleared his throat. "Roll 'im up," he said, and within seconds, two guys pinned the old-timer's hands behind his back and carried him away, while another two rolled his things together before following behind. "Roll that fucker up," repeated Lefty, "and tell the guards to send this geezer to Intake 2 with all the other faggots and queers."

The entire moment was empowering. Lefty and I bowed to each other and would later share the old-timer's weed and celebrate in the triumph. We-got-shit-done was how we acted, and although it was a small victory when compared to everything else, we held onto the moment because it was all we had.

"Here's my information," Lefty had said, handing me a folded piece of paper on my last day in The Ghetto. "You'll be outta here soon enough, an' if ya ever need anything, I'll do my best to help."

I thanked him and left him there, transferring to the second level, The JKL, where I earned the privacy of a cubicle around my bed and the comfort of separate-stall showers. It wasn't much, but I bided my time, spending my days in front of the television watching movies, reading the books I promised to read after graduating from college, and writing song ideas like I'd always done—only this time, without the assistance of my guitar.

My life was about imagination, and I used it to save my sanity. If it weren't for music, I would've eroded; and had I not written lyrics and notes in my notebook, I would've never taken my chances back in LA.

Growing up, I was always passionate about music, but when I entered high school, that passion took a backseat to my grades. Music was fine if it meant recitals and playing in the company of family, but to my parents who were poor, music was a step below the poverty line. They wanted a college degree, and they wanted something that could make a consistent paycheck. It's a familiar story, and I went along for the ride, but while they thought I was studying the books at UCLA, I was spending half my time at concerts and indie shows.

At the JKL (and later on at level three, the 124 Hilton), I'd sneak within earshot of the blacks and listen to them as they battled each other in daily rap contests. I never had the guts to join them, but from what I heard, I broke their verses down and tried to understand the meter and the rhyme. Music is a science, and you need to be an artist to understand it. The blacks at the Honor Farm weren't going to be famous, but they could rap because they had soul.

I figured, after all I'd been through growing up in Fox Creek, the fact that my parents were who they were, and everything I'd done as a loan officer, I had enough of the heavy heart that I could convince a man to listen to what I had to say. So when I finished my sentence, with nothing to my name except my savings account and a notebook full of scribbles, I took the cheap acoustic guitar my mother had bought for me in the Philippines and moved to Los Angeles, in Echo Park.

I was at the bottom, with nothing but my dreams to carry me back.

※

I received another phone call, and this time it was the husband. "Cali," he said, "it doesn't look good. We've increased the dosage and expect it to happen soon."

"I'm sorry to hear that."

"It's for the best. Miranda wouldn't have wanted to die with so much pain."

I left the fantasy woman in the morning and drove through Stockton, reminiscing about all the misadventures of my youth. The neighborhoods weren't like they used to be, and if you paid close attention, you could see the dividing lines between the subculture and the established culture. Everything outside of Lincoln, Quail Lakes, Spanos, and Brookside was left for dead and taken by the immigrants. When I left for college, North Stockton seemed like the perfect melting pot, but as I drove down Hammer Lane and onto West, I could see how the pot had become more Asian flavored than anything else. Except for the Costco, the Wal-Mart, and maybe the Baskin Robbins, there was no reason to visit the north side if you didn't belong.

The old joke in Fox Creek was that you never found dogs, only dog bones. The joke was funnier if you were from the neighborhood and bought your meat from the white rapist van that drove through the streets, going house to house, selling portions from the cow carcass the old Laotian lady chopped in the cab.

I remembered everything as I drove. From Kelley Drive to Eighth Street and back to North Stockton. Even the Bernay/Bordeaux quarter where my high school sweetheart lived.

She was raised in a traditional Cambodian family and was promised to some thirty-three-year-old with a fifteen-thousand dollar dowry; and because I was only a kid, and because I had no money, and because I was Filipino—and even worse, half white—our relationship was forbidden. Soon after our sophomore year, she married him and became pregnant, and the last I heard, they had moved away to North Carolina.

On the top of the lamppost, at the end of Bernay, the city installed a video camera to record all the criminal activity that takes place. If it had been there when I was fourteen, it would've recorded the black kid who asked for my CD player after he claimed to have a gun hidden in his coat pocket. "Give it up," was what he said. It could've been a pen he was holding, but because it was Bernay, I gave him my CD player and walked to my girlfriend's house.

If being born and raised in Stockton means anything, then it's been well-deserved and stolen.

I drove through most of the neighborhoods I could remember and passed by the duplex my parents called home. If my calculations were correct, my mother was sleeping after working the night shift at McDonald's, and my father was plugging away at the computer, playing World of Warcraft. And my sister? She still hadn't forgiven me for missing her high school graduation.

She had already moved out on her own, and even though we weren't "friends," I'd check her Myspace or Facebook to see where she had moved to. At that time, she was professing to live in San Francisco, but you never knew with Ramona. "I'm not gifted like you," she had said. "Graduating from high school might be the only thing I ever do."

I could've gotten her definite whereabouts from my parents, but it had been years since I last visited; and although I played with the idea of surprising them that morning, I went with my better judgment and decided to leave them alone. Seeing me would aggravate them and lead to a two-hour lecture about the wrong turns in my life.

◈

I stopped by Brookside and parked my truck within eyeshot of the house I had helped Luke Walker buy. The sign out front said the house was in foreclosure, and when the garage opened and out came Luke carrying a box, I thought about driving over to say hello.

His hippy father grew up with my hippy father, and to everyone with normal names it made sense that California Shock would be best friends with Luke Sky Walker.

He had resented me ever since he realized the subprime would kick in on his loan and he'd be forced out; and even though I tried everything to help him modify his mortgage, it didn't help either our friendship or his family.

I watched him pack his car and wave good-bye to the white picket fence and the American Dream.

◈

After driving for another two hours and using a quarter of my gas, I decided to buy some music at the old Tower Records, which had now become Rasputin Records. I parked my truck and entered, not knowing what I wanted, but knowing I wanted something. It was another five hours back to LA, and even though I stole most of my music from the Internet, I wanted something new, something original, something with a voice, a gem, a musician I could eventually meet and collaborate with. It was a lot to ask for, but I thumbed through the aisles and searched.

No one ever buys movies or CDs anymore, which I knew going in. My phone had iPod capabilities, but I never bothered to download music with it. The truth was, I missed those days when you had to drive to buy things. The weekly Blockbuster runs with Ramona, and those days when we'd bike to Tower for magazines.

The girl working the counter caught me staring at her lip ring and smiled as I passed by and continued to rummage. She could've been twenty-one, maybe twenty-two;

and by the way she presented herself, she was either a student at Delta College or a single mother. The cutoff T-shirt wrapped around her body like a loincloth, and whenever she needed to help a customer, I would stare at her breasts, at the way they nestled and shifted, the way she used them to her advantage.

"Will this be all?" she asked, after running the bar code of a Son House CD.

"Yeah," I said softly.

She had an esoteric look about her, like every worker at a Rasputin Records. She was heavily involved with either the punk or reggae scene, and if she didn't have an iPod, she probably had a vinyl player. She was the kind of girl who always knew the DJ, the girl who didn't need a Google search to find an upcoming show. That was the vibe I got from her, but then again, it could've all been a front.

I would've opened by mentioning my own music, but I didn't see myself in that light, so I smiled and paid for my purchase. "Have a good day," she said.

The Safeway across the parking lot looked enticing, and I figured I'd buy some snacks for the drive back to Echo Park. Perhaps a couple bottles of Gatorade, I thought, and a bag of jerky, or a bag of chips.

As I approached the front entrance of the Safeway, I caught sight of an old woman being mugged for her purse. She must've been around sixty, and her assailants were two boys, of medium height and build, running away with their skateboards and the woman's purse. "Help," she cried. "My phone. My credit cards."

We made eye contact. I'll admit, if that hadn't happened, and if she had been a man, I probably would've left it alone and walked inside. But as it was, the old woman, with her desperate face and the aching in her eyes, reached out to me as a final plea, and with neither police officer nor security guard in sight, I let instinct take control and gave chase.

I didn't say a word, but the boys heard my racing steps and sprinted back toward the record store, where the one lagging behind dropped his skateboard. *Fuck*, I thought, picking it up. They were headed across Pacific Avenue, zigzagging through traffic; and as I followed, I could see that the one who dropped the skateboard was the one with the purse.

He had the complexion of a punk, and every time he turned around, I could see his sneaky eyes and their apathetic feeling to all things educational.

My intentions were to take the purse and let them go. I didn't feel like being involved in a police report, so I prepared my words. We were now at the old Naughty Nick's parking lot, which had now become a gambling house.

Being steps away from the punk, I lurched forward with my stride and tackled him hard. The two of us rolled on the asphalt, my knees scraping through my jeans as I pushed the kid down and picked up the purse. I was out of breath, but able to talk. "Get out of here," I told him.

The parking lot was empty except for the section for the gamblers, and after I tucked the purse in my jeans, I bent down to pick up the skateboard, only when I did, I realized we were no longer alone. The faster kid must've run and grabbed the other friends who were hiding behind a fence somewhere.

They surrounded me with cruel intentions, all five of them with their fists clenched, including the punk kid I tackled, who now, because of the strength of the group, had the courage to spit in my face. F-this. F-that. F-you. He threw all the expletives in my direction and spoke as the majority, his cocksure attitude hitting me from every angle.

My adrenaline had risen in a matter of seconds, and the muscle memory of my youth resurfaced from deep within. I assessed the situation, counting the five in front of me while the punk kid continued with his insults. My addition was correct, and when I realized this, my eyes took aim, searching for the toughest of the group, who from looks alone, appeared to be the wannabe with the pencil-thin mustache and goatee. His slicked-back hair was a dead giveaway for the kind of kid who would do anything for the affirmation of his crew.

In my experience, idiots like him were the most dangerous. He'd have a knife inside his pocket—or worse. And if I stayed to find out, I wouldn't have put it past him to cut me in the liver. I needed to find my way. I needed to escape.

"What now?" yelled the punk. "Where you going, bitch?" He threw his hands out and invited a free shot. "You fucked up now, bitch. It's fucking over."

His friends were smiling and I knew we were moments from something. Of the five, I felt like only the punk and his goateed wannabe had the guts for a fight.

We were all about the same height and size, except for the portly one wearing the tight jeans that hung like an ice cream cone around his legs. He was bigger, but only because he was fat. Not an ounce of muscle from my vantage point. Running through him would be my exit strategy. Running through him and back across the street where someone could help was all I could think about.

F-this. F-that. The kid spit at me again, not realizing I had his skateboard in my hand. F-this. F-that. His lips sucked in to reload, but this time, instead of letting him shoot another loogie, I cocked his skateboard and loaded my hips with everything I had. And as sure as anything I'd ever done in life, I made damn sure to connect the trucks of the skateboard to his face, hitting him with such force that it popped a wheel off, sending it into the air as the kid's blood splattered from his nose and onto the pavement.

I had enough time to enjoy my work for a split second. His blood was gushing in chunks, like goo onto his cupped hands; he was no longer able to speak. The shit from his words stuffed back into his throat. He coughed, then gagged, falling onto his knees so he could catch himself from fainting.

"Oh shit," I whispered, and broke into a sprint toward the portly one, pushing him in the chest and gunning it back across the street.

The group was stunned, but I could hear them chasing me. I had improved my odds from five-to-one to a manageable four-to-one, and if I could just reach a group of adults, if I could just find someone who could help, then maybe I could side-step the ass beating and be done with it.

I crisscrossed through traffic just like the muggers and from there, I had to make a choice. Should I head left and run the two-hundred yards back to Safeway? Or should I make a right into the Chevron station beside Rasputin Records? The latter was the easier choice, so I crouched my head into my chest and pumped my arms, running past the gas pumps and into the Chevron, where I was caught by the goateed wannabe, who grabbed my shoulder as I spun around and threw a haymaker with my left arm, catching him awkwardly on top of his head, the two of us crashing into the aisle of potato chips and chocolate bars.

"Oh, my God!" cried the woman behind the cash register.

By the crunching sound my hand made, I knew it was broken. The other three arrived soon enough, and before I could get my bearings, they were pouncing on me, throwing kicks and stomps that landed all over my body. "Oh, my God!" I heard again.

My body curled into a defensive ball, and because of my experience with fighting, I kept my eyes open to see what was what. The slicked-back wannabe stood up and grabbed the coffee machine beside him and dropped it, the brunt of it landing on my shoulder; I was able to shrug most of it, but I knew I was moments from blacking out.

The wannabe kicked the hands in front of my face, then bent down to pick me up, taking my shirt into his hands. "Next time I see you," he said, "I'll fucking kill you."

He made sure we were face-to-face when he said it, and after he did, he pulled back for one more punch. By now, I was too weak to flinch. *Fuck it*, I thought. The blood raced into my mouth, and his punch connected and exploded through my teeth, my head landing against the cabinet beneath the slushy machine and coming to rest on the floor.

"You fucking chink," he said. "Go back to China where you belong."

When the police and ambulance arrived, they found me stooped on the sidewalk in front of the Chevron holding a bag of ice against my head. The wannabe and his crew were long gone by now, and as my mind fought the cobwebs, the police asked their questions. They were in the process of finding the owner of the purse, and up to that point, they only had the surveillance video from the Chevron to piece together the story.

My name was entered into their system and was met with a red flag. Not only did I spend time in the Honor Farm, but I was also affiliated with a local gang. "But I'm not a gang member," I said.

"It says here that you are."

I stared at the two policemen, trying to understand. They noticed my right hand and the tattoo printed on my knuckles. "What's that?" asked the first one.

"It's a tattoo."

"What's it for?" asked the second.

"I was a kid," I sighed. "I got it when I was sixteen."

They nodded and wrote some notes in their notebook, and I tried to explain that I was a nobody. "Is it against the law to have 2-0-9 on my hand?" I asked. "Dallas Braden has one, and he's a pitcher for the Oakland A's."

They said no, but they wanted answers. "So why does your name come up in our system?" asked the first. "You have a misdemeanor for vandalism, and you're connected. That's what we're trying to understand."

I told them any sort of affiliation occurred years ago, back when I was in high school, and only because they were my childhood friends. "Like I told you guys the last time I was arrested," I said, "I am not and have never been in any gang. I was invited to three parties during my junior year in high school," I continued. "And each time, the police were called because of a dispute, and because I was at each one, they categorized me as more than just a friend. Does that make any sense?" I asked.

They wrote more notes, and when the call came in to verify my story with the old lady's, they let the medics clean and release me. I didn't even get an apology. "Thanks," I said, as they took the purse and drove away.

The medics examined my hand and said it was broken. "Do you want us to take you to a hospital?" they asked, but I declined and began to walk. "I can drive myself," I said.

My face was covered in mosquito-bite welts and my bottom lip was warm from the blood. If I pulled my shirt off, I'd find more bruises, and if I opened my hand, I'd find the music career slipping from my fingers. "What now?" I asked, and started my truck.

※

The tattoo in question was the brainchild of impulse. My high school sweetheart broke the news to me right after first bell. "I'm sorry, Cali," she lamented. "But there's nothing more I can do. He already paid the dowry to my parents. We're getting married."

We were in front of the band room, and I was already late for guitar class. She cried her tears and hugged me, squeezing every ounce of my memory from her system, and when she finished, our hands lingered together, but then she let go.

A year later, I performed for the talent show in front of the entire school, and played a song I wrote for her, but as I sang and looked into her eyes, she was already married and pregnant. My words never changed a thing, and I swore to myself that would be the last time I dedicated anything to a woman, the last time I'd play a love song, the last time I'd fall in love.

When she left me in front of the band room that day, I decided to ditch school. I bumped into a friend from the neighborhood, and he asked me if I wanted to go with him to San Jose. "I feel like getting another tattoo," he said. "Want to come?"

The kid's name was He, but everyone knew him as He-Man, because he once fought a kid twice his size, using a metal lock between his knuckles to give him extra leverage. "The guy called me a gook," he said, and instead of expelling him, the assistant principal wrote it down as self-defense and gave He-Man a five-day vacation.

He-Man was walking to his car when we bumped into each other, and I was on my way to Carl's Jr. for some breakfast. It was either eat or get a tattoo. I looked down the street and thought about the meal I wanted to order, and then I looked at He-Man and thought about the tattoo I wanted to get. "I know a guy," he said. "He can give you one even though you're only sixteen. He tattoos all my friends. His name is Pinkie."

I nodded my head and walked with He-Man to his car. Back then, the high school attendance systems weren't as advanced as they are now; and because I could write my absence off with a forged note, it didn't matter anyway. We drove the two hours from Stockton to San Jose and arrived an hour too early. It was eleven, and Pinkie wouldn't be in until noon, so we drove to a nearby mall and ordered a whole pizza from the Sbarro's in the eatery and took it to a planter outside by the Macy's.

"What kind of tattoo do you want?" I asked.

He-Man took his shirt off and showed me what he already had. "Well," he said, "there's the black widow on my stomach. The dragon on my chest." He pointed and ran his hands across the ink. "I'm thinking about getting a web on the back of my shoulder." A woman in high heels passed by and dismissed us as two juveniles, and He-Man put his shirt back on. "What about you?" he asked. "What do you want?"

I picked at an olive from the pizza box and chewed on the question, thinking about the possibilities. Until then, I never thought about getting a tattoo. It wasn't like it is now, where getting inked is a birthright, and every girl dreams of the flower above her lower back. No. Tattoos were on the verge of the explosion, much like everything else, so instead of something big, I wanted a simple tattoo.

My favorite basketball team was the Chicago Bulls, and they were in the midst of their second three-peat. Scottie Pippen had a "Pip" stitched to his arm. *Something like that,* I thought. An expression that doesn't say much on the surface but leaves an aftertaste when you think about it. A piece of art that everyone can see and immediately know a little bit about me and what I stand for. "Something like that," I told him.

He-Man paused and finished his slice, taking a cigarette out for his dessert. "You want one?" he asked. I put my hand out and said nothing, and the two of us sat there, puffing away, neither of us knowing quite how to smoke but determined to know through practice. He was a senior and had picked up the habit after he turned eighteen.

"You know what I hate?" he said. "I hate that every movie is about New York, or Los Angeles. I hate that the only thing written about Asian men is written by Asian women who were never skinny or pretty enough to date their own race. I hate how every Asian woman is a victim, and we're supposed to be the reason." He scratched the side of his head, the cigarette stuck between his fingers. "We're reading *Joy Luck Club* in English right now, and all the Southeast Asian girls are talking about how hard they've got it, telling the teacher what it's like to live in Fox Creek." He put the cigarette back in his mouth. "I say, fuck that. If it's so bad, then why don't they just move out? I hate all of them, with all their college dreams and honor classes, thinking they're better than us. Shit. I hope they move out, because when it comes time to clean up Fox Creek, they ain't going to be there. It'll be us. Guys like me and you who'll have to do the grunt work."

I didn't have the heart to tell him Fox Creek would always be Fox Creek. He-Man was speaking about frustration, and not necessarily about Asian women. There was a pain deep inside him. It could've been the fact that he'd have to stay home no matter what and raise his little sisters. It could've been the fact that his parents took his paycheck from Taco Bell and gave him nothing back. It could've been a lot of things. A broken heart. A life going nowhere. I knew where he was coming from, so I let him speak.

"Let's get 2-0-9 tattooed on our hands," he said. "If we ain't ever going to get respect as Asian men, then we should just take it." He smiled and bobbed his head. "It's like you're telling people, this is where I'm from. This is my home. This is my house. And if you can't respect that, then this punch is coming from where I was raised. Coming straight from the ghetto and into your face." He nudged me on the shoulder. "You know what I'm talking about?" I did. "I'm talking about the only thing that matters when push comes to shove. It's respect, Cali. And the only way anyone will know about us, is if we put it in their face for them to see. You know? You feel? Cuz I'm not trying to disrespect where anyone else comes from. I just want everyone to know where I'm at."

We agreed and decided to get 2-0-9 on our hands, waiting in line behind a bunch of college kids from San Jose State, who were getting fraternity letters. "It's the kind of pain that makes you want more," said He-Man, and I wondered if he was still talking about tattoos.

Of course, years later, when I was at UCLA, and when representing your area code became the thing to do, I took the North Star from the NorCal symbol and put it on my pinkie finger as a compliment to the original. It's a bit macho, but a tattoo that means something is a lot scarier than the most decorated skull. I'd step in the ring with a guy covered in two sleeves before messing with a felon who had a tear drop on his cheek.

"It's all about respect," He-Man said. "And sometimes you have to take it."

We eventually lost touch after I left for college, but every time I look at my right hand, I remember that day and everything he said.

The doctor at Kaiser called it a boxer's break and put a cast over my left hand. The visit lasted the afternoon, and when I was released, I decided to drive back to Echo Park. I knew I'd get an earful from my manager, about how I had just thrown away my opportunity, so I was prepared for the worst. If the break failed to heal properly, how well could I play? If I was reduced to being just another rapper, or just another musician, would I ever get signed?

I exited off the 99 and used the cross-town back to the 5, heading south for Los Angeles. That wannabe and his friends were all I could think about. *How did I let this happen,* I asked myself. *In my own hometown, no less.* It's a changing of the guard when the young ones can step up to the old, but the way it happened was what stuck. The utter disrespect. The words they used and the attitude with which they did it. "Fuck them," I said, squeezing the steering wheel.

I became angry. I became enraged and manic. The kind of anger a woman would never understand. Born from all the lies I'd been dealt, from all the pain of being a man. From all the shit I'd taken from the world, and all the shit I'd take if I ever wanted love.

They took my dream away, and because a man without a dream is only a boy, I concluded that they were going to get theirs, specifically the wannabe with his goatee and slicked-back mullet. "How dare he," I said. "He doesn't know me. He doesn't know what I'm capable of." I slammed the cast onto the steering wheel and popped a Vicodin from the bottle the doctor prescribed.

This was a *Boyz N' the Hood* beating he had coming to him, with all the sick-twisted fantasies that came with it. Of a knife stabbing through his hand and into a dining table. Of watching him squirm to get away. Of slamming a plate into his face. Of forcing him to bite the edge of the table. Of me kicking the back of his head and breaking his mouth. *American History X* style, just like Ed Norton did in the movie.

I had just passed Eighth Street when I remembered that Lefty lived in Weston Ranch, aka Little Oakland. I had five seconds, and then I'd have to decide. Drive back to Los Angeles, or get some help and get my revenge. All my friends had either moved away or been locked away, so all I had was Lefty. "The hell with it," I said, and exited the highway, pulling my wallet from my pocket and reading the information Lefty had given me.

If the wannabe thought he could get away with this, he'd do it again; and to let him live in ignorance, I just couldn't do. I resolved that sometime between then and the end of the weekend, I'd find him and tell him who I was. "My name is California Shock," I imagined myself saying. "And if I see you in Stockton again, not only will you die, but…" my mind crashed in all the heinous things I could say, and instead of finishing the thought in words, my imagination drove to the finish, taking me into Weston Ranch and into Lefty's driveway, where I found him cooped in his garage, working on a 77 Celica. A real man, doing man's work, drinking a man's beer. Everything I wanted to be, and everything my father wasn't.

"Holy shit," he said, when he saw me walking. "Mr. Shock." He remembered me, and with my face slightly dismantled and my hand a broken mess, his smile transformed, and by the way I was holding the paper that held his information, he knew what I was there for, and he knew what that meant. "Z," he said, referring to his Hispanic friend beneath the Celica. "Grab 'im another beer. I want ya to meet a friend of mine."

※

For an hour we caught up like college roommates and mused over the time we shared at the Honor Farm; and after drinking four Coronas, I broke down and told him everything that had happened. "These kids," he said, "ya think they're in high school, or college?"

"Neither," I said, "but I'm pretty sure they're adults."

"How can ya tell?"

"I don't know," I replied. "Just by the way they talked." I took the bottle opener and popped another beer. "It doesn't matter," I continued. "I don't care if they're in high school or junior high. If you can drop a coffee machine on another man, then you're old enough to reap his revenge."

Lefty looked at Z, who was a quiet migrant about my age. They nodded to each other and smiled. "Makes sense," said Z, speaking with a Mexican accent. "If you did it, then you did it."

The garage across the street opened and out drove a red Mercedes. Lefty motioned us to be quiet and stood up from his chair. "Here we go again," he said, and the three of us watched the Mercedes pull onto the street and park, the driver's door opening and releasing a petite Chinese woman in a matching red dress. The look on her face told of an immigrant misinterpreting the American Dream, the confusion of correlating price with class. Her heels clinked against the pavement as she bent in front of the Mercedes, pulling at the bumper, not knowing how to fix a car, a damsel in distress. "Excuse me," she said. "Excuse me."

Lefty wiped his hands on his jeans and approached the woman. "Can you fix this?" she asked. "Henry say it broken. He say it need fix." She put her hands out and tilted her head to the side. Her body was too thin for her frame, and her face too thin for her head. She was twenty pounds away from beauty, and by the way she carried herself, she would never know.

As the two of them spoke, Z pulled me aside and explained the situation. "Henry found her on the Internet," he said, "and flew all the way to China so he could marry her." We both took a sip of our beers and watched. The little woman was trying to convince Lefty to fix the bumper, but Lefty wasn't having it.

"I ain't gonna stop hangin' out with my friends so I can fix this," he reasoned. "It'll be okay. You can fix it later."

But she continued to persist. "You sure?" she kept saying. "I no want to die. I scared of dying."

Lefty raised his eyebrows, befuddled by her words. "You'll be okay," he smiled.

"You sure you can't help?"

"Like I said before, you're askin' me to stop talkin' to my friends so I can fix this. I'm drinkin' with my friends." "You'll be fine," he said.

They stared at each other, waiting at an impasse. She eventually bent low again, prying at the bumper, and Lefty took it as his cue to turn around and return to his chair. "You'll be fine," he said, and the Chinese woman retreated to the driver's side and sped away.

Henry, the husband, had married a bipolar maniac, and it made you wonder why. "They talked for about two hours," said Lefty, "an' then she convinced him to take her to the courthouse, an' then she convinced him to get married."

The Chinese woman had been living in Henry's house for a year, and he soon found what he had paid for. The woman was smarter and crazier than she led him to believe. Her scheme was an elaborate plot to accuse him of physical abuse, to have him arrested and then divorce him—but only after she took his car, his house, and his money. "Henry isn't home," said Z, "because he's out looking for a lawyer. He said he never touched her. He said they never had sex."

"Can you believe that shit?" asked Lefty. "How the hell do you marry someone, you bring them to America, an' for a year, you don't get nothin'?" He finished the last of his beer and repeated himself. "Not a single thing."

The question took us back and we all arrived with the same answer. "Fuck that," we said, speaking like frustrated men. She had Henry by the short and curlys; and even though I didn't know the man, and even though I thought he was an idiot, I felt bad, as we all did. "If that were me," chimed Z, "and I flew to China and brought her to America, she would've already had my baby."

Henry should've just found a woman in America. "But then again," said Lefty, "the poor bastard was lookin' for somethin' on the traditional side. A wife who could cook. A wife who could care for an' massage him after a hard day's work. A woman who knew her place an' not only accepted it, but enjoyed it."

"They don't make them like that anymore," I said, and they both agreed.

For three hours that led into the night, we chewed on Henry's situation and came to the conclusion that he needed to deport her. And it wasn't until we got hungry that we were able to change the subject and return to normalcy. In struggling neighborhoods like Weston Ranch, there's no shame in eating and hanging out in an open garage, so I sat in my lawn chair and watched Lefty and Z pull the homemade barbeque grill and cook the steaks they were defrosting for dinner. "I made it from a barrel," Lefty proclaimed. He yelled for his wife and introduced her, along with his two daughters, who were nine and seven years old. "So let's talk about revenge," he said, when she and the family departed back into the house. The three of us, Z, Lefty, and myself, huddled together, scooting our chairs close.

"I don't care about anyone else," I said. "The only person that matters is the wannabe."

"Well if they're skaters," thought Z out loud, "then they should probably be at the skate park off of El Dorado."

"So we get there tomorra an' we find 'em," added Lefty, "an' then what? Exactly what kind of revenge are you lookin' to get?" He slid his hand across his neck. "Do ya wanna kill this guy?"

I laughed at first because I thought he was joking, but neither of them cracked a smile. "No," I replied, and cleared my throat. "I mean, I don't know. I just, for some reason, really need this. I need to have the last say."

They finished their steaks by holding the last bits like bread, soaking them with barbeque sauce, and as they swallowed, they tried to see the revenge through my eyes. I had been beaten and knocked out, and they had taken a part of me I needed back. Our methods for revenge escalated with the suggestion of weapons. For Z, a bat was enough, but for Lefty, who owned a mini-arsenal that he inherited from his grandfather, a bat just wouldn't do. "I want to keep it as close to legal as possible," I said, "but I want to make sure we get him."

We settled on golf clubs and decided to scout the skate park in the morning.

⁂

Because he only had two bedrooms in his house, Lefty gave me the girls' room and made his daughters sleep with him in the master. The bunk bed was small, and the walls were decorated with rainbows and unicorns, and the bed sheets were stiff, smelling like they had just been bought and never washed. It was uncomfortable, but I had no choice. "Everythin' okay?" Lefty asked.

I pulled the blankets from where they were tucked into the mattress and fanned them, releasing the stale air inside. "I'm good," I said, and stretched into a sleeping position.

He licked the steak stuck between his teeth and told me it'll be fine in the morning, and then he closed the door. The clock by the lamp read a little after midnight. Because I had taken another painkiller, I thought I could fall asleep, but for whatever reason, I could do nothing but stay awake. The darkness ignited the glow from the stickered stars on the ceiling. I stared at them, imagining they were real. It made me think about a lot of things, but mostly it made me think about Jay Warner, my old boss, because if I had stayed with him, I would've followed him and become a real felon.

I checked my phone and searched the Internet for the latest on his case, and after reading the comments in the news articles from the Sacramento Bee, I realized that not much had changed. Jay Warner had been pinched because of the Ponzi scheme, but the FBI wanted his thirty-six-year-old cohort, Douglas Clark, who was the mastermind behind the swindle. "If only," I said, running my thumb on the touch screen.

Jay Warner agreed to testify against Douglas, and as the Feds began to build their case, Jay Warner chartered a private jet to Las Vegas and lived the rock star life for a week before taking the jet to Tel Aviv. The Bee said he and another passenger used fake passports, and when I read on,

I speculated about whether he was now living a new life. If I had stolen that much money, that's what I would've done. Jay Warner was a criminal, but I had to give it to him—he had balls.

❦

My phone vibrated and I opened the text message. It was the fantasy girl. "*Hey,*" she said. "*I just wanted to say hi.*"

I tried to ignore her, but the messages kept coming. "*I thought about you today,*" she continued. "*So when can I see you again?*"

She probably thought that because I didn't text her all day, it meant I was playing it cool and casual. Women mistake neglect for maturity, so I kept my responses short and sweet. "*Too bad you're not in Stockton,*" she wrote. "*I'd be down to meet up again. But oh well.*"

I looked at my phone and scanned the room around me. I was one click away from being with someone. About an hour from smelling the lotion lathered to her shoulder blades and kissing the dimples on her back. The text message said I was "*…actually still here,*" and when I sent it, I sent it without hesitation.

"*Really?*" she replied.

We could've gotten things rolling if I would've just called, but since their inception into popular culture, text messages, for the simple fact that it keeps a dated record, thus leaving little if any wiggle room for a man to speak his way out of a conversation, have become the preferred mode of communication. The fantasy girl was no different, and after twenty minutes of hammering out the contract for a second rendezvous, she decided to meet me in Weston Ranch.

I scrolled through my phone and sent a message to Lefty, telling him that a woman was on her way to meet me, and like a true friend, he responded like a brother. "*Okay*," he said.

I sent the fantasy girl the address, and she in turn Googled my position and found me at Lefty's. "What happened to you?" she asked, when she saw my face. I walked outside the house and met her on the sidewalk, just as she was about to lock her Prius. "Did you get into an accident?" she said.

"I'm okay," I replied and gave her a kiss. She tasted like cigarettes, and her jeggings left little to the imagination. She smelled like a caricature and only through time, would she ever smell real.

The fantasy girl grabbed my hand with her perfection and led me back into the house, as if I were the one who had driven to meet her. And if it was sex that we wanted, it would have to be quiet. After laughing about the rainbows and unicorns, we snuggled into bed, her hips digging into mine while mine ground into hers, our bodies warming the bed from the chill I had left it with. "This is so weird," she said. "I feel so cheap."

We laughed again, and then I told her to slow down. "I just want to lie here for a second. It's been a crazy day," I said. She continued to laugh, but soon it faded into a giggle; and before long, we relaxed and fell silent, our bodies wrapped into each other, her face breathing into my chest, while my face breathed into her hairline. The girl even slept beautiful, I told myself. But if it ever got serious, she'd probably cheat. It would only take a bigger name to sway her, but I knew I was right.

I didn't know if I could keep her attention, so I took charge of the moment and turned her body, pulling her pants down so that she was only wearing her T-shirt and socks.

The day I became a man was the day I realized sex is just a garnish.

I entered her quietly, both of our eyes closed, imagining a better tomorrow. When we woke up, hours later, I made her leave through the window. "I'm sorry," I said. "I can hear the children watching cartoons." Her jeggings got caught on the window and ripped at her thigh. She gasped and glared at me. I was wearing nothing except my boxers.

The fantasy girl stepped onto the grass and pointed her head into the sky. The dew had sunk into her shoes, and when she turned to show me, she gave me a look that said we'd never be naked again. But when she entered her Prius, our eyes connected a final time, and we both knew it wasn't over. This was a blossoming courtship that had all the makings of a relationship filled with antitrust and fights that threatened a breakup whenever the words boiled beyond comprehension. The exact relationship we had both sworn to stay away from, but always seemed to fall into. "*Is your life full of drama?*" my message said. "*Because my life is drama, and I don't need any more drama in my life.*"

The fantasy girl replied with a no, and because I knew she was lying, she had taken another step away from being the fantasy from her Facebook page. In my eyes, I now looked at her as only Kelly.

⁂

I changed into my clothes and decided to call the husband. The phone picked up, but it was silent. "Are you there?" I asked.

"I'm here, Cali."

"I'm out of town right now, but I hope to make it back tonight."

He sniffled and said they took the CD of the Brazilian song I made. "And we've got it on repeat," he said. "I don't know how much longer, but it'll be soon." His voice sounded fragile.

"Is there anything I can do?"

"I don't know, Cali. I knew this day would come, but it feels so quiet now. I already miss her."

◦◈◦

After his daughters left for school, and after his wife left for work, Lefty opened the bedroom door and told me to get up. He stood and waited for me to gather myself and said not to bother pulling the sheets from the bed. "Them girls never sleep on the bottom bunk," he said. "They like sleepin' together on the top."

I followed him through the hallway and took a seat in front of the kitchen table, where he offered me a cigarette and a cup of coffee. "You take any sugar or cream with that?"

"Yes," I replied. "Both, please, and lots of it."

Lefty drank his coffee black, which explained the hoarse and forcefulness of his voice. He threw some pastries into the toaster and we ate breakfast together, mixing the sweet with the bitter, and filling the air with smoke. "I figure I'll drive and we'll pick up Z at his house." I put the coffee mug to my lips and drank, watching the cigarette stick out from my hand. "It's Friday, so maybe there's a chance they'll go there today. I mean, shoot, I doubt these kids have jobs." Lefty rubbed the stubble beside his jaw. "The only thing is, is that we might have to wait there all day. Ya sure you want this?" he asked.

"For the last time, yes," I replied. "And for the last time, I don't want *them*; I want the wannabe with the slicked-back hair."

Lefty nodded and took his keys from the change bowl beside the counter, and we walked into his garage, where the 77 Celica sat, waiting for repairs, and where another car waited, a series of blankets masking its true identity. "I never showed this to you, yesterday," he said. "But this is my baby."

The black 67 Chevelle shone without a crease, and its tires polished with gloss. The car was kept in mint condition for Sunday drives and special occasions; Lefty said we'd probably need the trunk space. "That's why we're takin' mine instead of yours."

We pulled away from the driveway, the engine gurgling an angry spitfire, and headed to pick up Z, who lived twenty minutes north in Lodi.

※

As soon as I became a senior in high school, my father drove me to the McDonald's on 99 and Kettleman Lane, where my mother worked, and made me fill out an application. I wanted to work as the pianist at the Nordstrom's in Sacramento and practice my Chopin, but because I wasn't eighteen, they wouldn't let me apply. "My first job was at McDonald's," my father said. "Everybody should work at McDonald's, so they see what it means to earn a living."

I wasn't a big fan of his, and so I asked him what for. "It didn't teach you anything."

He would've punched me, but he didn't know how. By the time I left the manager's office, I had been interviewed and hired. I was an official crew member, part of the Ronald McDonald family.

Aside from the Indian kid who was working to pay for his Berkeley tuition, there was no one else headed for college, and because of that fact, they put me behind the register. I was the one people looked at before they ordered, and after a month on the job, I had the stereotypes down. Of course, the more experienced workers warned me about this, but when I first started, I didn't think it could be true. "Whenever you get a Mexican," they said, "he'll probably order a Big Mac. But remember, you need to clarify it with him. Sometimes they say Big Mac, meaning they want the Big Mac meal, and sometimes they say Big Mac, meaning they want only a Big Mac. And if you get an Indian," they'd add, "basically someone who looks Middle Eastern or whatever, they're probably going to order the fish fillet. With them, too, you have to remember to ask if they want the meal." Asians, I learned, were a little harder to pin down, but the most annoying were the white people and the fat people.

The white people were annoying because they always wanted a special order. If the customer was a housewife, the odds were high that she would order a cheeseburger for her son, but without onions, or with half the cheese, or without pickles. And this was before they changed their policy to making the food when ordered. No, no, no. Back then, the cooks were ordered to prepare food in bulk, to keep the bin filled with burgers and Big Macs. So whenever these special orders came in, it could slow things down and Little Miss Housewife would have to wait impatiently for her five hamburgers, where God forbid you get a burger wrong and add onions when you were supposed to add lettuce. She'd complain to the manager and want you fired. Which didn't bother me, since half the time I worked there, I dreamed of getting canned.

I guess that was the most annoying part of the job. The fat people weren't as bad, but you kind of felt sorry for them because of their delusion. For them, it was an extra value meal, supersized, with extra mayo, but a Diet Coke, because they were watching their diet, or because they were diabetic.

The worse part of the job came from the workers themselves. At the one where I worked, we had five mail-order brides from the Philippines, with two of them acting as shift managers and the other three as crew members who dreamed of becoming managers. I told them when I was hired that I didn't want any shifts with my mother, so they put me in the shifts with the crew member brides, which was a disaster from the start. They suspended me because I made the youngest bride cry one day because I told her she was basically an idiot.

Her name was Magdalena, and what separated her from the pack was her innocence. When I think about it now, I realize I probably went too far, but I was a kid, and I didn't understand why someone would leave their family, marry some stranger, and work for minimum wage. That kind of logic didn't make sense to me.

"So how do you like America?" I asked her.

"It's fine."

The lunch rush had just passed and we had some down time to talk. These were questions I had always wanted to know but could never ask my own parents. "So how did you meet your husband?" I eventually asked.

She responded with her accent and danced around the question, and I wouldn't let go. "Be serious with me," I said. "Be honest. You met your husband through a service."

We argued this point for a while, and while she didn't admit to it, she tried to convince me of her love. "He's a very good man," she said, the tears cracking in her voice.

"But you just met him," I reasoned. "I don't understand how you could be in love with someone you just met. How could you fall in love with someone who wants to take you to America? Is it really that bad in the Philippines? Were you really that poor?" The tears were visible now. "Why would you come to America and not go to school? What about the boyfriend you had back home? What happened to him? Was it worth it? Did he not make enough money for you? Were you that selfish?"

My mother suspended me for a week, and when I returned, I realized I was done with the place. So when a little boy returned his Happy Meal toy three times because it wasn't the right one, and when he complained that there were onions in his cheeseburger, I waited for the boy to walk away. Then I grabbed a barbeque sauce packet and threw it at the kid's head, hitting him on the neck, the barbeque sauce exploding in every direction while the boy cried to his grandmother. "This is an outrage," she exclaimed, and I looked at the two of them and said, "Tough shit," dropping my crew hat and walking out to the parking lot.

Both incidents soured the relationship with my parents, and we were all happy when I left for college.

Lefty drove from the 5 and headed east onto Kettleman Lane, and as we passed the 99 intersection, I leaned forward to see the McDonald's parking lot. My mother, in her manager's outfit, was walking to her car, her face pointed down like always, watching and counting her steps. I waited to see if she would look up, but she didn't, and we continued east and into a subdivision for migrant workers.

Z stood for Zepeda, and during the drive, Lefty explained his friendship with the man, saying he hired Z to paint the Chevelle, and since he had done a good job, they became friends. "But don't let his quiet demeanor fool you," he said. "Z can fight. He's like a pit bull when it comes to that stuff."

I laughed and said, "That's how I know I'm back home."

"I don't get it. Explain."

"In LA, and even in college, whenever you want to know about someone, you ask what their major is, or what job they do."

"Okay," nodded Lefty.

"But in Stockton," I said, "when it comes to guys like me and you, if you want to know about someone, you find out how tough they are, if they can handle themselves in a fight."

"That's jus' how it is, Cali."

I stretched my arms out as we approached Z's house. "I bet you have a story," I said.

"Sure do," replied Lefty. He smiled and looked at me. "The guy got in a fight one day, was gettin' the snot beat outta him, and so, instead of takin' his beatin' like a man, Z grabs the guy's head an' bites the tip of his nose off." He bowed his head and stared at the road. "I asked Z why he did it, an' he said he needed to win. So if you're worried," Lefty said, "don't be. The three of us should be able to handle these punk kids, no problem." He reached under his seat and pulled a Glock 22. "An' if worst comes to worst," he said, "we could always take it up a notch."

We parked seconds later and waited for Z to come out. He was a married man, with four children who were in high school; and with four graduations around the corner, he was always hustling for money, doing paint jobs and maintenance work when the time permitted. He didn't look much bigger than five foot; in fact, you could've sworn he was taller when he was sitting down, but I knew better. When a man like Lefty vouches for a guy, it's legit. Z locked the front door to his modest duplex and walked to the Chevelle carrying a backpack and the set of golf clubs we agreed to use. "The farmer gave it to me when he bought a new set," said Z, "but I don't ever use 'em." He buckled his seat belt in the back and opened the backpack. "I made some tamales jus' in case we get hungry."

"Save 'em for when we reach the skate park," said Lefty. "We'll need 'em then."

We drove back west, retracing our steps to the 99; and this time, when we passed the McDonald's, I didn't bother to look. The Chevelle broke south on the 99 and exited Hammer Lane to fill up with gas at a Shell station. The three of us said mostly nothing and listened to the radio. I thought about canceling the whole affair, but with the golf clubs, the tamales, and the black Chevelle, I leaned back and kept my mouth shut. "Getting revenge," a friend once said, "is a rite of passage bestowed only to the most worthy." I shouldn't have been surprised by Lefty and Z's willingness to help. We turned left onto El Dorado and made our way to the skate park in Anderson Park, parking our car in the Mayfair Shopping Center. It was only ten and not a single kid skating. "An' now we wait," said Lefty. "Now we wait," repeated Z.

"Have you done this before?" I asked Lefty.

"Done what before?"

"You know," I shrugged. "Have you waited for someone like this before?"

He motioned for Z to throw him a tamale. "Yeah," he replied.

"How about you?" I asked Z.

"Of course, fucker," he said. "All the time."

As we waited, Z fell asleep, and I gave Lefty some money to buy beer at the Super King. "High Life," I said.

My stomach growled moments later, and I became hungry. I turned my head and poked Z in the shoulder, who was snoring in the back. "Give me a tamale," I ordered.

He wiped the saliva from his lips and tossed me the wrapped meat.

"Do you have anything to drink?" I asked, and he threw me a bottled water. "Thanks."

Z turned and searched the parking lot. "Where's Lefty?"

"I gave him money to buy us a couple cases of Miller High Life. He's at the Super King"

"The champagne of beers," said Z.

❦

The skateboarders trickled into the park as the afternoon set in, and each time a new face arrived, they asked me, but it was never them. "No," I'd say. "He's too skinny."

The restlessness took hold of Lefty, and he needed to do something, so he popped the hood and started to fiddle with the engine. "Cali," he said, "can you hand me a beer?"

We loitered around the Chevelle and talked about the kid we were hunting. "I bet he don't have any parents," said Z. "Kid like that got no respect for authority."

"I'll tell ya what it is," added Lefty. "These kids forget about today before it's tomorra. They got no sense for history an' who came before 'em. They think whatever is now is what was only."

I nodded yes and walked to the backseat for another tamale, listening to Lefty's rant.

"Take movies for example," he continued. "These kids today think *Star Wars: Episode I* is a better movie than *Episode IV*." Z disagreed. "But they do. They do, my friend." Lefty put his hands out and counted his fingers so he could get his argument straight. "An' not only is the original a better movie, it ain't even close." He inhaled to repeat himself. "It ain't even close."

"So that's why these idiots beat the shit out of me?" I asked. "Because they like Darth Maul more than Luke Skywalker?"

Lefty put his finger up. "No," he said. "It's jus' my way of describin' the type of animal we're dealin' with."

"And what kind of animal would that be?"

"Well, for starters, you could throw out every argument at these kids an' they'll stick to their guns an' say the new trilogy is better. But the real reason why they don't appreciate the original trilogy is cuz they don't appreciate the writin' an' the dialogue." Lefty squeezed his hands into a fist. "It's all about explosions an' special effects. The kids could care less about that clever line when Han Solo gets into the carbonite, cuz these kids don't talk to each other anymore."

"You can't blame them," I said. "Most of them were never alive when the original trilogy was playing."

"True. True. You're very true there, but that's still no excuse." Lefty began to scratch the side of his neck. "I mean, you ain't seen me arguin' about the greatest baseball player of all-time. I know, you know, we all know it's Babe Ruth. An' even though I've never seen him play, I can look at the record books an' concede that he is. An' so likewise, these kids, with their Internet and YouTube should be smart enough to watch the original three an' see how great they were. Episodes four through six was, and is, an' will always be the greatest trilogy of the series, perhaps the greatest trilogy of all-time." Lefty shrugged his shoulders. "That's what's wrong with this generation. The setting matters more than the story."

"You got no argument from me," said Z.

I laughed and looked to see who was at the skate park, and when I saw the fat kid I pushed from the fight, I took a bite of my tamale and paused. Should I run now, I thought. Should I tackle him?

The face was unmistakable, and now, without the pressure of being jumped, I watched the kid and saw him for what he was, which bordered on pathetic and lonesome. If he was the one who bought those clothes, then he must've had bigger problems at home. The fat kid looked lost and in the midst of an identity crisis. He walked with stiff legs, but that could've been because of his jeans. They were tight and they pushed his stomach fat above his hips. A layer of muffin skin hanging like expanded yeast. The shift from side to side. Over and back. Like a tube of toothpaste. The fat kid waddled to his friends, and after greeting them, he readied himself for a run, pressing his skateboard to a lip along a wall.

"Speaking of Darth Maul," I said. "There goes one of those fuckers right now."

"Who?" they asked.

"That one, right there. The one with the tight jeans and the black Rocawear T-shirt. That kid tipping his skateboard into that drop."

"Just him?" asked Z. "You don't recognize anyone else?"

I waited to see how the fat kid would do, and to my surprise, instead of eating cement, he made the drop and executed a few turns. His friends and the kids around them didn't look familiar, so I told them no. "I don't think they're here."

Z reached into the backseat and was prepared to grab a golf club, but Lefty told him to wait. There were too many bystanders, so we posted in front of the Chevelle and pretended to work on the engine. "What now?" I asked.

"I don't know," said Lefty. "It's your party. You tell me."

I put my hands on the fender and leaned into the hood and peered with my peripheral at the fat kid. Of the group that beat me, he was the least of my worries, making it hard to conjure the hate to do him wrong. His eyes carried an innocence behind them, which made him likable, and watching him socialize with the other skaters, I could see the potential he had, as did Z and Lefty, who by their indecision and the tone of their words were reluctant to hurt the kid. "You sure that's him?" they asked.

"Yeah."

They waited for me, and I remained still. I hadn't thought the plan through and expected the moment to be more of a reaction and not so much thinking. Maybe because he was so much younger than me, maybe that stopped me. I wanted his friend more than anything else. "Then let's wait for the wannabe," said Lefty.

"But what if he doesn't come?" I asked. "I don't want to waste the day, but I don't want to cause a scene, at least not with Fatty. It's not worth it," I said.

It would be a gamble to wait for him to go home, we decided. That could've taken an hour, or maybe three. Did we want to play that game, we asked each other. And what if he doesn't go home? What if he walks home with someone else? We didn't want anyone involved that didn't need to be involved, and from what we saw at the skate park, the group we wanted was absent. If the kids I stopped from the mugging were there, I would've grabbed a golf club and finished what they started. If the wannabe was there, it would've been worse.

I kept my hands on the fender and my eyes on the engine. "I want the fat kid in the car," I said, "and I want to have a private conversation. Whatever we need to do to make that happen, then let's do it."

Lefty took my words and opened the driver's side of the Chevelle, reaching underneath for his gun. Not like that, I wanted to say, but I stopped myself and watched. It was the kind of crazy-white-man look born of growing up as a hunter, of 4-H club meetings where he learned to gut a deer, of a guy tattooed to his tool belt, of hands and fingernails dipped in engine oil. "That's all you had to say," he said, tucking the gun into his pants. His steps vibrated into the ground and he made his way from the parking lot to the grass and into the skating zone.

When we heard his words, they were anything but faint. Lefty marched straight into the small group of skaters and pointed his gun at the fat kid. The action surprised everyone, including Z, who grabbed me by the arm and slammed the hood of the Chevelle. "Did ya get in a fight yesterday?" Lefty yelled. "Did you and your friends beat up a man?" The questions froze them, and Lefty slammed the butt of his gun into the fat kid's cheek. "What are you waitin' for?"

he asked the skaters. "Run! Get outta here! Get the fuck outta here!"

Z took a seat on the driver's side and I took shotgun. "Start the car," I told him. "Drive onto the grass and get next to the entrance."

With the skaters running around the Chevelle, Lefty seized the bleeding fat kid by the back of his shirt and dragged him into the backseat of the car. "Hurry up," said Lefty. "Drive east. Take Hammer Lane an' head for the 99. We'll hide somewhere in the cuts." The fat kid covered the gash on his cheek and the blood leaked through his hands. He moaned and cried, his eyes closed, as Lefty threatened worse if he bled onto the upholstery. "Go ahead an' try it, faggot. You jus' go ahead an' try." The fat kid opened his eyes, and the two of them stared at each other. "You bleed into your hands an' into your clothes," said Lefty, "or you ain't bleeding again."

The fat kid's breath sprinted in and out, and when I turned to look at him, the shock became terror and he cried some more, stuttering through mumbled words. "That's right," said Lefty, slapping the gun against the kid's head. "You start a war, an' we finish it." The car sped onto Hammer Lane, screeching against the asphalt, and swerving until all was clear. Lefty tucked the gun back in his pants, and for the hell of it, he punched the fat kid in the face.

I turned around and kept my eyes on the two of them by staring at the rearview mirror, popping a painkiller from the bottle in my pants. The three of us checked for police, and with not a single one in sight, the Chevelle slowed with the pace of traffic and headed east, past West Lane, past Costco and Wal-Mart, and over the 99, making a left on the frontage road. We came to a halt at the abandoned Morada Market, which wasn't quite in the cuts, but good enough.

Z cut the engine, and the three of us exited the car, pulling the fat kid aside and setting him down on a parking island. We all felt bad for him, so to make him feel better, Lefty threw him a rag from the trunk and told him to clean himself. The blood was everywhere, from his hands to his shirt, and when he was finally able to compose himself, we asked for his name. "It's Sean," he hesitated. "Sean Malone."

I knelt in front of him while Z and Lefty stood behind. "Do you remember me?" I asked. "Do you know who I am, Sean?"

He nodded his head. "Are you going to kill me?"

My first impulse was to play with his mind, so I ignored his question. "How many times did you hit me?" I asked. "When you and your buddies were stomping the shit out of me, how many hits did you get in?" Sean turned his eyes away. "Come on, kid. Add up all the kicks and the punches you threw."

"It wasn't my fault. I didn't start it. I was just, I was just going along with everyone else. I didn't mean to hurt you. Honest, I didn't."

I raised the cast and left it inches from his face. "Do you see that?" I asked. "You broke my hand, Sean. You and your buddies broke my hand, and now my future is in jeopardy." He began to breathe heavily, the tears coming in snot bubbles. "I play a guitar for a living, Sean. And now I can't play."

"I'm sorry," he whispered. "I'm sorry. I'm sorry."

"The good news is that we don't want you, Sean; we want your friend, the one with the goatee, the one with the slicked-back hair, the one who dropped the coffee machine on my shoulder." The fat kid nodded his head. "What's his name, Sean? His full name."

"George. George Thiessen."

Lefty bent down and reached into the kid's pockets and took his phone. "If he's tellin' the truth, the kid's name'll be in here." Lefty pressed the buttons to search, and when he realized he needed a code number, he handed it back to Sean. "Unlock it." The fat kid put the rag on his lap and did as he was told, handing the phone back to Lefty, who couldn't find the number. "He's lyin'," he said. "I ain't seen a George on his contact list." We waited for an explanation. "An' so?" asked Lefty. "You wanna tell us what's goin' on here?"

The fat kid sniffed and spoke. "It's under Gio," he said. "It's his nickname."

Lefty scrolled through the names and when he found it, he showed me the screen. "You know if you're lying to us," said Z, pointing to Lefty, "this old man is going to hurt you." The fat kid closed his eyes and bowed his head. "Was there anyone back there at the skate park who knows this Gio?" asked Z. "Would any of them call him and tell him what is happening?"

Sean's chest rose and sank, his eyes scanning from left to right as he thought about the question. "I don't know, maybe."

Lefty bent down again and put his hand behind Sean's neck, and with his other hand he cocked back for a punch, the phone still in his grasp. "You've gotta do better than that, Sean."

"Well, they weren't there. None of them. Because…" The fat kid sniffed for more. "Because they were headed to Davis for the weekend, all of them, the ones that jumped you. They were headed to Davis for Picnic Day."

"Picnic Day?" asked Z. "What the fuck is Picnic Day?"

"It's a campus party held at the end of every school year," I said. Lefty looked at me and wondered how I knew. "I had friends that went to UC Davis," I recalled. "And every year, they'd invite me to Picnic Day. It's basically an end-of-the-year drunk fest." Z and Lefty raised their eyebrows. "But it doesn't happen until Saturday."

"They wanted to get there early," added Sean. "There's supposed to be a party at someone's apartment. They're staying there for the weekend."

"And when did they leave?"

"This morning. They all left this morning."

"And why aren't you with them?" asked Z.

"I'm only eighteen," he said. "They said they were going to hang out at some bars." I scratched my head and asked him if they were all twenty-one, but they weren't. "They have fake IDs," he said. "They're all nineteen except for Gio. He's twenty, I think."

"Exactly how many of them are there?" I asked.

"There's six of them in all, but I don't know if anyone else followed."

I stood up and looked at them. "Well. I guess they're in Davis. You guys got any ideas?"

"Yeah," said Lefty. "I've got a couple."

We paused and waited for him to continue his thought, but he kept it to himself. "Well, spit it," I begged.

Lefty cleared his throat and bent down a third time, taking the rag from the fat kid's lap. "If we're goin' to finish this by tonight," he said, "roll 'im up."

I never went to Picnic Day during my undergraduate years; the first time I went to Davis, was with Jay Warner after work. He had some things in the Sacramento branch that he wanted me to do, and when I was done, he took me downtown and bought me dinner at a Japanese restaurant called Mikuni. It was a Wednesday night, and all the yuppies wearing ties and suits were mingling for happy hour, and I could tell Jay was unsatisfied. "Let's do something," he said. But I thought we were. "I mean, let's go out," he insisted. I surveyed the restaurant and wondered if it was because we looked young. What was it, I wondered.

Jay Warner had the novel idea that because it was fall and the incoming freshmen in most universities had just arrived that Sunday, we should drive to either Chico or Davis and meet something young. "But we don't have any change clothes," I told him. "We'd stick out."

It was a minor inconvenience, according to Jay, and after driving to the Arden Fair Mall and buying a set of casual clothes from Abercrombie and Fitch, we were off to Davis, taking the 80 west and crossing the causeway, exiting Richards Boulevard. "Why do I get the feeling you've done this before?" I asked.

"I never went to college," he said. "So for a while after high school, I'd drive to Davis, or Berkeley, even Stanford for the hell of it, and see what it was all about."

I shook my head and asked him what he found, and he told me the first week of college was his favorite. "That's when all the virtue begins to die," he said. "They're finally out of the house and they have to figure it out for themselves."

The wind stole the words from his mouth as his Mercedes convertible drove through Davis, and I didn't know whether to feel sorry for him for being such a creep, or to feel sorry for me because I chose to follow him. We were young enough to qualify for graduate students, so I excused our intentions, but as I watched Jay drive, I could tell and wouldn't have been surprised if he continued this college tradition into his mid-thirties.

His plan was to party at The Graduate, a pizza restaurant by the dorms that turned into an eighteen and older club on Wednesday and Thursday. "It's like this," he said. "This is the first night these kids are going to party. They've been getting ready for class since Sunday, and even though Thursday is the first day of school, they've been in their dorms, waiting for this night and the ensuing weekend." We were sitting inside his Mercedes, snorting a few lines, and he pointed the freshmen out. "See," he said. "That line outside The Graduate is going to fill with students any second now. The line will wrap around the building, but look to the right and see *that* line." He pointed to an empty line guarded by a couple of bouncers. "That's the line for all the twenty-one and older kids." "Watch how they're allowed in for free, and watch how many guys walk through that line," he said, smiling. "Not a single girl coming through. And that's because this is tradition. This is what they do. It's like high school, only worse."

"And how do you know this?" I asked.

"I've been doing this since I was eighteen."

We wiped the cocaine from our noses and approached the twenty-one line, handing our identification to the bouncers, who seemed as if they were holding in a smile they wanted to share with us, as if they knew who we were and why.

The situation would only spiral from there, and when we entered the restaurant, Jay Warner guided me to the left and into a boxed off area next to the bar. It was dark except for the occasional blinking lights, and if I wanted to talk, I'd have to almost yell because of the music jetting from the speakers. We were surrounded by other men, men who might've been undergraduates, men who might've been posing like us. Our conversations shrouded the fact that we weren't listening, that we were drinking our drinks and waiting for the freshmen to enter.

It was sickening to say the least, but after a few shots, and after watching the girls, who dressed as if they knew what was happening, I slowly relinquished my inhibitions and let the wave come over me. Jay Warner was a millionaire by all accounts, and because we were in Davis, scamming on the freshmen girls, I knew that it didn't matter. We would always be proles. We would always be common people. Which meant that girls were either bought or tricked, or even both.

We were destined to steal our money through folly, because we were never bright enough to inspire or smart enough to create. We wore suits and ties to work, but we might as well have been dressed as clowns. Money can buy many things, but it can't mask the stench of a creep.

If a dance club was an example of how the world works, I knew right then that I'd always be dancing. I'd never be good enough to own a private booth. I'd always be the pretender, the guy who had to buy the expensive bottle, never good enough on my own merits, with my own name.

So I did what I was supposed to do and pounded the last of my fourth tequila shot and made my way through the crowd and into the middle of the dance floor, where for a second, I stood motionless, waiting for the world to drop on its edge, the youth around me sweating their innocence away.

It only took two minutes for me to find someone, and when I did, I captured her arm because I could, and pulled my lips to her ear, asking her if she wanted to dance. She backed away at first to look at my face, and when she approved, I cupped her waist into mine and lost myself in the music, the sweat coming in rain drops from my pores and mixing with the sweat on the tips of her half-covered chest.

The freshman could dance, so I let her wrap her web and danced, waiting for her to discard me, but when she didn't, I pulled her closer and breathed into her ear, letting her taste the alcohol from my lips. "Let's get out of here," I said. "Where do you live?"

By now, I had built the story of lies, and she saw me as a graduate student who lived in Sacramento. The freshman had her own room, and because it was her first week of college, she did what she was supposed to do, taking my hand and leading me to her dorm. She claimed to be of Colombian blood, and by the build of her shoulders, she was either a soccer or softball player. Her ass carried the stiffness of a teenage erection. I kept my hands on it because I had never felt a woman so fit. "Do you like it?" she laughed, but I said nothing and pushed her into the bed. The freshman whispered and said the RA lived across from her, and we continued to kiss.

Her jeans fell first, as did mine, but when the foreplay ended, I touched below her waist and felt something I hadn't felt since high school. "What?" she asked. "Is something wrong?"

"No, no," I replied. "I just haven't seen pubic hair on a woman for a long time." The comment embarrassed her, nearly killing the mood. But I didn't mean it that way. I was drunk and fishing for something I couldn't find, and as I missionaried our bodies, she reached for her desk drawer in search for condoms, giving me time to check my phone for any messages from Jay. *"Where are you?"* his text asked. *"I'm at the south end of campus. Meet me back at my Mercedes when you're done."*

It was the first and only time I'd ever go to The Graduate, but not the first and only time I'd be with the freshman.

She seemed captivated by my lies, and for a while, you could say we were dating. The second time I visited her dorm, she surprised me with a shaved vagina, and I met her expectations with my own approval.

Was it wrong; what I was doing? Was she also at fault? We lost contact after I went to jail, and after my release, I tried to surprise her with a visit, but by then, the lies of man were transparent and she rejected me with a kiss and told me to never see her again.

Men are judged by the carnage of broken hearts in their past, and if there is enough, she will trust him to break hers.

Only after my experience with the freshman was I able to see what Jay Warner was after. He had never, with all his money, touched anything real, and he thought he could find it through the lie he was living. If I admired him for having the guts to steal his fortune, I did the same when it came to stealing love. "If we didn't do either," he once said, "someone else would."

We wrapped the fat kid's wrists and ankles with duct tape and tossed his body into the trunk, pouring beer on his face whenever he squirmed. "I'm sorry!" he yelled. "I'll never do it again! Please! Please…" Lefty peeled the duct tape from the roll and taped his mouth shut, closing the trunk and lifting the fat kid into darkness.

"It'll be okay, Sean," he said. "You're gonna make it out jus' fine." Lefty turned and sat against the bumper, pausing to hear his muted screams and opening the fat kid's phone yet again. "Let's see what else this kid has," he said, but just as he was about to scroll through his texts, the phone vibrated with a message from Gio. "*Hey*," it said. "*I heard the guy from yesterday was looking for you. What's going on? Are you okay?*"

Lefty raised the screen to our eyes and let us read the words. "What should I say?" he asked.

Z and I looked at each other. "I don't know," I said. "If we respond now, he might call the phone."

"But if we don't respond," said Z, "he still might call the phone."

We gathered together and watched Lefty. "*Yeah*," he typed. "*They tried to scare me but everything is fine.*"

"*Really? What did they do?*"

Z lifted his head and asked, "What now? What did we do?"

"*One of his friends had an Airsoft gun and pretended it was real,*" typed Lefty. "*He hit me with the gun and dragged me to his car, but then they pushed me out before they left the parking lot.*" He rubbed his fingers together after it was sent and asked if the message sounded real. "It should work," Lefty assured us. "I doubt he'll call back. These kids never call each other."

"*Damn,*" the message read. "*Are you sure you're okay?*"

"*I'm cool. Don't worry. The guy and his friends were laughing the whole time. They thought they were funny.*"

"*That's not cool, bro. That's not cool at all. Should we go back to Stockton and handle this?*"

Lefty read the message and showed it to the rest of us. "Perfect," he said, and turned to pop the trunk, the afternoon light hitting the captured body. "Yes or no," continued Lefty, speaking to the fat kid. "Tell us if you live with your parents. If you don't an' you're tellin' a lie, we'll do unspeakable things to you. Ya understand?"

Sean squinted his eyes and tried to use his eyebrows to cover the sun. Yes, he nodded, he understood what we were looking for.

"So do ya live with your parents?" Lefty asked.

He nodded again, saying yes.

Lefty slammed the trunk and returned to the buttons. *"No, it's fine. I'm actually back home with my parents. We can handle it when you get back from Picnic Day. I'll call you when I'm done or maybe later tonight."*

"Sounds good."

Lefty closed the phone and put it back in his pocket. "That takes care of that," he said. "So what now? Shall we head for Davis?" He circled to take the driver's side, and I followed by taking shotgun while Z buckled in the back. The Chevelle sped out of the abandoned market and took the frontage road onto the Morada Lane onramp, heading north on the 99.

⁂

We were no more than ten minutes out of Stockton, and I could tell there was something on Lefty's mind. His lips twitched into silent words as he spoke to himself, and his body rocked back and forth, his eyes frothing at the lids. We would've caused an accident had I let him continue, so I tried to break his concentration. "It's a good thing that Gio kid didn't call the phone," I said, trying to congratulate his gamble.

He continued to rock back and forth, except he turned to understand my statement. "A good thing?" he asked. "You think it's a good thing?"

"I mean…"

"No, Cali," he interrupted. "It ain't a good thing."

Lefty was agitated, and he let me know, moving his eyes between myself and the road, all the while rocking his body, his blood pressure on tilt. He squeezed the steering wheel and swallowed, and I waited a few seconds to see how long he could keep the pace, and when he had settled, I told him that I wanted to know what he meant. "But I'm afraid to ask."

His eyebrows lifted into an expression, and he turned his attention back to the road. "I knew Gio wouldn't call," he said, "cuz that's the type of kid we're dealin' with." Z, who had an arm stretched across the backseat, leaned forward and rested his elbows between us, against the front seat. "It's like the Star Wars argument I had back there at the skate park," said Lefty. "Technology ruined this generation, an' not only do they not appreciate history, they don't know how to talk to each other."

"You're starting to sound like an old man," smiled Z. "Don't you think you're being a little hard on them? They're jus' kids."

Lefty put his right hand up. "They ain't kids," he said. "Don't give 'em an excuse. Don't give me that shit, Z." Lefty ran the hand through his hair and put it back on the wheel. "It's either ADD or ADHD or some other learnin' disability. I can't pay attention. I can't remember. These kids got more excuses and nothin' to learn."

"I can see what you're trying to get at," I said. "But what exactly is your point?"

"There's jus' somethin' about this generation of kids," he said, using his hands to drive and speak. "All these kids born in an' around 1990 have no sense of anythin'."

I waved my hand and asked him to explain.

"It's like this," nodded Lefty. "I live in Weston Ranch, an' for the last twelve years or so, I've noticed fewer an' fewer kids playin' outside. I ain't seen anyone playin' a neighborhood game of stickball or football or even basketball." He shrugged his shoulders and turned into the slow lane so he could gather his thoughts. "Play time is either done through Little League or Pee Wee Football or online, an' what you've got is a kid who doesn't know how to socialize in a natural setting."

"You don't think you're overanalyzing this?" asked Z.

"No, I'm not. An' what I'm gettin' at, what my point is, is that we now have a generation of kids that don't understand what it means to lose, an' to overcome losin'." I looked at Z, who looked back at me, mouthing that he didn't understand. "They get a trophy for finishin' in tenth place. They think their feelin's deserve some weight. They think that messagin' a girl over the Internet means bein' a ladies man. An' they think they're somethin', when they really ain't." He wiped the saliva from his mouth. "An' I knew that Gio kid wouldn't call me cuz he didn't have time to talk."

"Maybe he didn't have any minutes," said Z.

"No, buddy. The kid had minutes, an' the reason it ain't a good thing that he didn't call is that we now live in a world that's separated in reality, but together in fantasy."

"That's pretty deep, Lefty," I said, "but what does any of that have to do with us, or the fat kid in the trunk?"

"Everythin', guys. Everythin'." He coughed into his hand and cleared his throat. "If these fuckin' kids had been raised properly an' been dealt the leather of a belt whenever they fucked up, there's no way they would've robbed that old lady. There's no way they would've jumped you an' injured your hand." He nodded his head and watched our reaction. "They would've understood what it meant to respect their elders. They would've learned a lot of things about life."

"Like what?" I asked.

"Like what it means to be a friend, an' what it means to help a friend out." He checked the rearview mirror for traffic. "If this situation was happenin' to me, not only would my friends have called, they would've dropped what they were doin' an' driven back to Stockton an' tried to beat the shit outta whoever had the guts to trunk their friend. But these kids," said Lefty, "they're probably more concerned about the party. They're more concerned about havin' sex an' drinkin' alcohol, an' takin' pictures so they can put 'em on the Internet." Lefty nodded and stepped on the gas, overtaking the big rig in front of the Chevelle. "They've got a hundred friends on Facebook, but they don't know what it means to be a brother.

"An' I bet you this," he continued. "I bet you that not only is that fat kid a Star Wars fan, but I guarantee he likes the new trilogy better than the original."

"You're that sure?" Z laughed.

"I bet you," said Lefty, pointing a finger into the air. "These kids, cuz they don't understand the real world, would never appreciate greatness. They can only see in black an' white, cuz they can't think critically. They can't *see* critically." He pushed his blinkers and took the Elk Grove exit. "It's like lookin' at music an' sayin' that cuz that new kid, Justin Bieber, cuz he has more number one hits than Jimmy Hendrix, is a better musician."

The Chevelle turned into an empty section of a parking lot beside a Denny's restaurant. "What are you doing?" I asked. "We're supposed to go to Davis, not Elk Grove."

"Watch," said Lefty, putting the gear in park. "I bet you this kid's an *Episode I* fan." He motioned for Z to hand him a golf club, and after he got the putter, he stepped away from the car and walked back to the trunk.

"Is this guy serious?" I asked Z.

"When it comes to kids?" he replied. "He's always serious."

Z and I met Lefty at the trunk. He popped it open and waited until the sunlight entered into the cabin. Sean's eyes were closed and he appeared half-asleep, and as he stirred and refocused his eyes, Lefty pointed the end of the putter into the fat kid's groin. "Wake up," ordered Lefty, and pulled the duct tape from his mouth. "I need for you to answer a question."

Sean sniffed the snot in his nose and looked down at the putter, trying to understand our motives. "What?" he asked. "What now?"

"It's like this," said Lefty. "If you answer my question correctly, I won't hit you with this putter." The fat kid closed his eyes and sighed. "You get what I'm sayin'?"

Sean opened his eyes and acknowledged the question.

"Ok," Lefty paused. "Answer this riddle." He coiled the putter back like a cue stick in a pool game. "Who, in your opinion, is a better Jedi knight: Darth Maul or Luke Skywalker?"

"Are you serious?" the fat kid asked. He began to huff and puff, waiting for the putter to strike. "Are you fucking crazy?"

"Now remember, Sean, before you answer my question, Darth Maul was a badass who looked like a demon an' had a red lightsaber that shot out of both ends. But then again, you've got Luke Skywalker, the leader of the Rebels, an' the savior of the galaxy."

The fat kid sniffed again and spit the snot into the trunk. "Fuck you," he said, his voice screeching into a high pitch. "You fucking-crazy-cocksucker. I'm not going to answer your stupid question." He sniffed the snot a third time and spit into the trunk once more, which made Lefty even angrier.

He wanted his answer, and he fought the impulse to beat the kid with the club, clenching the putter until he realized it would do no good. "God damn it," he said, pulling back and slamming the trunk shut. "He doesn't wanna answer my question," Lefty whispered.

"Well what the hell did you think was going to happen?" I asked. "You put the golf club next to his junk and you expect him to answer? Of course he won't say anything. The kid is scared."

"I have to agree with him," added Z. "Maybe if you offered him something, maybe he would answer."

I wanted to stop Lefty, but I couldn't. He was bordering on fanatical, and with the gun, the car, and the fat kid in the trunk, the situation could've escalated within minutes. Lefty looked like a man possessed—of a relic in search of a meaning. "Okay," he said. "I'll cut the kid a deal." Lefty popped the trunk back open and pointed the club at Sean. "If ya tell me who's better, we'll take ya outta this trunk an' set you in the backseat."

The fat kid wiggled his wrists against the duct tape and blinked a few times. The blood from his cheek had dried and the nervousness from his forehead ran into his eyes. "Will you let me go?" he asked.

"Eventually. But only after we get your friend."

Sean exhaled and told us his answer. "Luke Skywalker," he said.

Z and I turned to see Lefty, who withdrew the putter and pulled the kid out of the trunk and into a sitting position against the bumper. "Good answer," he said.

Lefty reached behind Sean and took his wallet from his back pocket, taking his driver's license and reading the information. "You understand that we know who you are, but ya don't know who we are," said Lefty. "So if I cut this duct tape from your wrists, you ain't goin' to try anythin' funny, are you?"

The fat kid nodded. "What about the tape on my ankles?" he asked. "Are you going to cut them too?"

Lefty reached into the trunk and picked up a beer, handing it to Sean and ripping the tape from his wrists. "No," said Lefty. "We're gonna leave it."

✦

Taking our original seats inside the car, we led Sean into the backseat of the Chevelle and let him taste his beer. His hand shook as he sipped his drink, the nervousness resulting from the men who watched him. He swallowed carefully and waited for the ignition to turn, but we remained fixated on the fat kid and noticed the stain and smell from his jeans. Sean followed our eyes to the source and took a breath. "I got scared," he said. "I had to pee, but I couldn't do anything because of the tape."

The mixture of blood and urine saturated the air, and the three of us coughed, hoping the smell would fade, but it didn't. "What now?" asked Z. "The smell is a little strong."

Lefty ran his tongue across his teeth and without a response, he started the engine and proceeded to pull out of the parking lot. I thought we were headed back to the highway and on toward Davis, but Lefty took the overpass and turned right and into the Wal-Mart shopping center. "You're not serious, are you?" I asked him.

"I am," said Lefty, and stopped the Chevelle, parking in the back lot of the Wal-Mart. "If we're gonna have the kid with us, we can't have him lookin' like piss an' shit." He turned and observed the fat kid. "We'll get pinched for sure if we don't buy him some clothes, an' before you know it, we'll be charged with kidnappin'." Lefty motioned to Z, who took it as a signal to get out, and when Lefty stared at the two of us, he handed me the gun. "Tuck it in your pants," he said, "an' only use it if ya have to." He grinned and spoke to Sean. "Like I said. If ya have any ideas of runnin' away from us, we'll find you." Lefty pointed a finger at Sean's head. "It might not be today. It might not be tomorra. But mark my words, we'll find ya. Do you understand?"

Sean's eyes looked away, but he knew his place and understood the situation, and after Lefty received his answer, he gave me the keys to the Chevelle and told me to call him if anything unusual happened. "Bring the car around," he said, "an' we'll meet ya at the entrance."

I slid over to the driver's side and watched Lefty and Z walk into the Wal-Mart, positioning my back against the door and my legs across the front seat, keeping half my attention on the fat kid in the back, who seemed uninterested in the drama, his mouth yawning with fatigue, the blood and urine drying against his skin. We were quiet for five minutes before one of us said a word, and when the silence was broken, it was Sean who spoke first. "I lied to your friend," he confessed. "The truth is that I don't care about Star Wars; I'm a Harry Potter fan." Sean coughed into his hand and continued to drink his beer.

My phone vibrated with a text, and as I pulled it out to read the message, I asked him how he did it. "How did you know to answer with Luke Skywalker?" I said. "Were you just guessing, or did you know something?"

"I was just guessing," replied Sean.

The text message was from the 4-1-5 area code, San Francisco, and it asked me if I was in Los Angeles or still in Stockton, and because I knew my sister and how she could never keep a phone number or a phone, I assumed it was her and told her I was in Stockton. "So how do you know him?" the fat kid asked. "Are you guys part of some syndicate or biker gang?"

I squinted my eyebrows at his question and told him he had watched one too many movies, and then my phone vibrated again. "*I know it's been a long time since I've talked to you,*" the text message said, "*and since everything that happened, I know I'm the last person you want to see, but I was wondering if you could pick me up at the Dublin Bart Station.*"

My sister was no stranger when it came to asking for favors. She had been blessed with the blood of Caucasian and Filipino parents, and because the genetics matched so well, she was beautiful, which allowed her to get whatever she wanted. Boys never had a chance in high school, and now that she was an adult, neither did men. She could've gotten a boy to drive her to school, and she could've gotten a man to buy her a car. Ramona didn't have to work on her personality the way normal people did; and in many ways, I resented her for this.

It was true that we both shared the same parents, but for some reason, I failed to inherent her gift. Ramona had the olive skin of a model, the cheekbones of an unforgettable smile, and hair that would've looked thick and stunning regardless of color. Where I, on the other hand, if I could describe my looks, was more like a hologram, like one of those special baseball cards. I could've been this. I could've been that. But I was never completely one thing.

"*I'm busy*," I typed. "*Ask someone else.*"

"*Are you serious?*" the message asked. "*After all we've been through, you can't pick me up? I rarely ask you for anything, and considering all that we've been through, I would think you'd at least pick me up this one time.*"

The tone was a bit harsh, something I hadn't seen before in Ramona, and my initial reaction was to block the number from my phone and continue my conversation with Sean, but I took a breath and realized it was my sister. She hadn't forgiven me for missing her high school graduation, and now that she was finally reaching out to me, I couldn't take it for granted, so I told her to calm down. She still owed me about five-hundred dollars from the time I paid for the Justin Timberlake concert her and her friends flew to in Arizona, but I wasn't going to bring it up now. "*I'm taking care of some things,*" I replied, "*and if you really need my help, I won't be able to pick you up until later tonight.*"

"*That's perfect,*" the message said. "*I won't be in Dublin until after midnight tonight, so be there before one. I'll pay for your gas and give you a little extra. After everything, I'm glad we're still friends. Thanks, bro! You won't regret it.*"

What was my sister into, I thought. Was she a stripper? Did she work at one of the clubs on Broadway? Or was she in the Tenderloin? I imagined what the last couple years must've been like for Ramona; and although being a stripper was my greatest fear, I wouldn't have blamed her if that's what she decided to do. A beautiful woman's curse is that she should be rich before she is old. Ramona had nothing to offer except her looks. She matured in those immediate years after high school, and I sat there in the Chevelle, wondering what mistakes she committed along the way.

"Who is it?" asked the fat kid.

"Who's what?"

"The one texting you."

"It's my sister," I said. "She wants me to pick her up."

"But you can't," replied Sean, tasting his beer, "because you're about to beat up some kids."

I smiled and put my hand out, and after he swallowed, he passed me the beer. "I told her I was busy," I said, and took a drink, finishing what was left. "My sister thinks I'm always going to be there for her, so she takes advantage when she can."

"Tell me about it. I've got a little sister who just started high school this year, and she's already talking to a senior, even though she's only fourteen."

"You've got a sister?" I asked.

"I've got two," said Sean. "The other one is in sixth grade, and she's already taking after her older sister. They'll be pregnant and married before they turn twenty-one. I just know it." He laughed and ran his hands through his hair. "You wouldn't happen to have a cigarette by any chance, would you?"

I felt my pockets out of habit and checked the glove compartment and found an unopened pack of Marlboro. "You're in luck," I told the kid, and unwrapped the pack, bumping two sticks and giving one to Sean. The car lighter was ready minutes later, and after I sparked mine, I lit the fat kid's cigarette and sat back against the door. "So tell me," I asked him, "why is a guy like you friends with guys like them? I mean, you seem like a good enough kid. But why would you befriend these jokers? You're better than that, aren't you?"

Sean puffed on his cigarette and said he could blame it all on his father. "He told me to make friends with the cool kids."

"What does that mean?" I asked.

"I guess my father was picked on when he was a kid, seeing as how he was fat like me, and he probably didn't want me to suffer the way he did; he figured I'd be better off with the slackers instead of the nerds. At least that's the way I see it." Sean saw me staring at his face. "What?" he asked.

I was looking at the gash on his cheek. "Your face," I said. "Does it hurt?"

Sean blew the smoke from his lungs and touched the cut. "No," he said. "But I bet yours does." He pointed the cigarette at my face and took a glance at the cast on my hand. "I hope you know I didn't mean anything by it. I only kicked you a couple times."

"Thanks," I smiled. "I'll remember that."

Sean tapped the ashes out of the Chevelle, and I got up to open the trunk for another beer, taking two and giving one to Sean.

When Lefty and Z returned, they were holding a bag full of clothes. "We didn't know what size you were," said Lefty, "so we guesstimated an' figured these would fit best."

"What the fuck is this?" asked the fat kid, pulling the jeans from the bag. "Is this supposed to be some kind of a joke?"

"They're called pants," said Lefty. "An' they're supposed to fit comfortably around your waist. We shouldn't be able to tell whether or not you've been circumcised. An' that goes for tight jeans an' baggy pants." Sean was in shock and couldn't believe he'd also have to wear a regular sized T-shirt. "We also got ya some bandages an' ointment," continued Lefty, cutting the tape from Sean's ankles. "So when you're done cryin' about your life, you can go ahead an' fix your face."

We converged outside of the Chevelle and allowed Sean to change his clothes, and as we waited, Lefty shared his thoughts. "When we get to Davis," he said, "we should text this Gio kid an' find out where exactly he's spendin' the night. It's college, so there's probably some kind of party, an' if so, we'll meet 'em there an' finish this thing tonight."

"What about the fat kid?" asked Z. "It's too much trouble to haul him here and then there. The boy has served his purpose. We should leave him somewhere or something."

"He's right," I said. "We don't exactly know what will happen in Davis, and if we keep him with us, something bad could happen."

"But I disagree," shrugged Lefty. "We keep the kid 'til it's done. Cuz for all we know, he could walk to a payphone an' call his buddies an' warn 'em, an' then what? We've got a real fight with no end." He began to gesture with his hands. "They call their friends," he said. "We call our friends, an' it jus' turns into somethin' it ain't supposed to turn into. No, no," continued Lefty. "We keep this kid 'til we know for sure where this Gio is."

"But that means we'll have to take the fat kid with us wherever we go," I said.

"No, no," he repeated. "We keep 'em in the backseat 'til we get to Davis, an' then when we know for sure where this Gio is, we'll roll the fat kid back in the trunk an' leave him there 'til we're done."

Z pinched the bridge of his nose and nodded his head. "It makes sense," he said. "It makes perfect sense."

We all turned to check on Sean, who was done changing, and when we returned to the Chevelle, Z took the original clothes and stuffed them in the trunk. "Now that's more like it," commented Lefty. "Now you look like a proper young man, like someone who's gonna do somethin' with their life."

The fat kid rolled his eyes and adjusted the bandage on his cheek. Then he tilted his beer and drank until it was gone, placing the empty bottle on the floor between his feet. The Chevelle no longer smelled of urine and blood, and from the outside, we looked like four friends on their way to an eventful Friday night. Sean's body language gave a hint of frustration mixed with hope. He must've wanted nothing more to do with us, but he knew and we knew that his freedom depended on the whereabouts of his friend.

His face still vivid in my mind as we drove north toward Sacramento. The name *Gio* kept repeating itself, along with the story of the fight. It was a step-by-step recollection, as I replayed it and tried to figure an alternate scenario. Should I have just ignored the old woman? Should I have let the security guards handle it? Or maybe I should've yelled and waited for someone to save me. Or just ran to the gambling house, where I could've found sanctuary amongst the pit bosses who probably lived near Fox Creek and would've recognized me as one of their own. The scenarios were many, and I stared at the road, thinking about them.

We were stop-and-go with the Friday traffic; the roads bottlenecked with commuters heading back to Sacramento and travelers on their way to Reno and Lake Tahoe, and before we hit Sacramento, Lefty smacked his lips together and told us he was hungry. "Then eat a tamale," offered Z, but Lefty was tired of Mexican food and said he wanted McDonald's.

"Does that work for everyone?" he asked. "Or do you guys wanna eat later?"

I shrugged my shoulders, as did Z, and when Lefty looked at the fat kid through the rearview mirror, he laughed. "Don't bother answerin'," Lefty said. "We already know you're hungry."

The clock on my cell phone read twenty minutes after five, and I had to check it twice to believe the afternoon had passed. The sun had begun its descent into the west, and as a result, the air, the grass, and the reflection seemed to reflect an orange glare. Lefty flipped the radio to The Eagle 96.9, and when Lynyrd Skynyrd's *Free Bird* rolled through the speakers, the four of us said nothing, riding the beat into Sacramento, our heads bouncing with the rhythm of the drums and the trill of the guitar as it swelled with momentum and drowned the percussion of the piano. "Cause I'm as free as a bird now," we lip-synced. "And this bird, you cannot change." We were all friends for the ten-minute duration of the song, but after it ended, the bond receded into the undertow of the speakers. For a few minutes, Lefty tried to recapture the tide. His hands worked the radio buttons, searching for another anthem, for a song to return the moment, but by then we were already exiting and turning into the McDonald's off of midtown.

I stared at my left hand and tried to wiggle the knuckles stuck in the cast; the pain throbbed with each movement. Lefty pulled into the drive-thru, and after posturing for a second, he put the Chevelle into reverse and backed out and into a parking space. "What are you doing?" I asked.

"I'm parkin'," he said.

"And I can see that, but why are you parking? We don't exactly have the time, and in case you have forgotten, we have a prisoner in the backseat."

Lefty ignored my statement and asked for his gun. "I'm hungry," he said, tucking the Glock in his pants. "An' if the kid has any smart ideas, I'll shoot 'im."

◈

I wasn't particularly hungry, but I ordered a Big Mac, while the other three all ordered a Quarter Pounder meal with Coke. We took the table next to the back entrance, and if Sean thought about running away, he did a good job of hiding it. There were numerous chances to make a break for it, from the walk into the McDonald's to the moment before we ordered, but Sean continued to play along, as if we'd been friends since forever. It's because we're in McDonald's, I thought. The fat bastard is hungry, and that hunger trumps all other thoughts. I watched him take a bite of his burger, and then I watched him eat his fries with two hands, using his left to reach inside the box and passing the fry to his right before taking a mouthful. His hands were coated with oil and salt. "What?" he asked. "Do you have a problem?"

The front entrance opened, and in came two police officers, who smiled at us as they proceeded to the counter. Lefty and Z responded by taking a look at the fat kid, while I did the opposite and watched Lefty's hands, which were creeping back to his waistline, in search for the gun. "This burger is good," said Lefty. "It's a shame I'm full; otherwise I'd eat it all up." It was his lame attempt at normal conversation, and it failed to calm either of us.

I kept waiting for Sean to raise his hands and run. His eyes rotated from the officers, then back to his meal and over to his captors. And this is it, I told myself.

The policemen took their order to go, and after a few minutes of talking to themselves and filling their cups with soda, they told the manager good-bye and left the McDonald's without incident. It was Sean's only chance, and I asked him why he hadn't taken it. "You could've turned us in," I said. "Why didn't you?"

"I don't know," he replied. "I guess I was scared you'd shoot me."

We stared at each other and when no one said anything in return, I took the Big Mac from my tray and continued to eat. The sesame seeds from the bun crunched inside my mouth, and I chewed the meat and the secret sauce until nothing was left in my hands. "You should've ordered a meal," said Sean. "Now you're going to ask for our fries and a taste of our drinks."

"You sound like you eat at McDonald's all the time," said Z. "Maybe it's wise that you just let him have some of your leftovers."

"What leftovers?" asked Lefty. "This kid ain't ever had a leftover in his life."

Sean raised an eyebrow and mumbled at the comment. "I didn't mean anythin' by it," continued Lefty. "I was jus' jokin'."

"No, you weren't. You meant every word."

"How do ya know?"

"It's in your eyes," said Sean. "You guys look at me like I'm some kind of loser. You think that because I'm fat, I won't be able to make it in life. And you know what?" he went on. "You guys are wrong, and you're just…" He bit his lip. "You're just projecting your failures on me. Just like the way you'd do if any of you had kids."

"Look at the balls on this guy," said Z. "You got a lot of nerve."

"But you're wrong," replied Lefty. "We ain't projectin' anythin' on you. We're jus' critiquin' Generation Y, as in, 'Why me? Why can't I seem to get my life goin'? Why can't I ever get a girlfriend?'" Lefty wiped his hands clean of the French fry salt and took a sip of his Coke. "When I look at you an' kids like you, I see a lot of wasted potential."

"Oh, God," I said, rolling my eyes. "Not another lecture."

Lefty raised his hand in my direction and told me to wait. "This is somethin' he has to hear," he said. "If we can't beat this kid an' leave 'im for dead, then I'm gonna make for damn sure he fixes the error of his ways." His hand drifted away from me and landed in front of the fat kid. "The problem with your generation is that you don't ask any new questions. The problem with your generation is that we tried to hand you the future, but you guys rejected it an' ran away from the responsibility. Generation Y?" asked Lefty. "If you ask me, the Y is ironic. An' if you ask me, the problem comes down to this." He pulled his hands together and mimicked a miniature globe. "The world rotates today cuz in the past, men could see the forest from the trees. They could put aside the pain, knowin' it was all for tomorra. But you guys, you guys can't see it anymore. No, no," said Lefty. "You couldn't bribe these kids with the future."

The fat kid sat quietly, shaking his head, and when he realized Lefty was done, he wiped his mouth and said, "The problem with your generation is that you had your chance to get it right, but you didn't. And now you see what you've created, and instead of taking the blame, you spend your time living vicariously through us and criticizing the life you always wanted but never had."

⚜

If I was going to pioneer and develop a genre of music that fused folk with rap, the trick wouldn't be in the rapping or the rhyme scheme of my lyrics. Rapping, at its core, is a series of simple rhymes, but the difference between a rapper and a wannabe is the ability to convince the audience. For rap music to be believable, the subject matter must be one that the rapper has experienced. In my case, although I lived in an area influenced by urban ideals, I felt my guitar would provide a different lens and take rap and folk in a direction never seen before, at least not at a proficient level. And in order to pull it all off, I needed to develop a voice that could back up my words.

With the studio I built in Echo Park, I spent eight hours a day inside my room, working on my sound; and by bouncing from job to job, I used my unemployment checks to pay for my rent. It was a Frankenstein operation I had going in my room, where for days, I'd study the voices of musicians and figure the recipe for my voice.

For the simple fact that rap-rock is a fast version of what I was after, I went straight to Zach De La Rocha of Rage Against The Machine and transferred the music into my acoustic guitar—which was easy, because I understood music theory. You first must figure out the melody, and from the melody, you figure out the bass line, and from the bass line, you can find your chord progressions. And when I slowed the tempo, I could hear Zach's voice and understand why it worked.

A rapper can't have a smooth tone. He's got to have creaks and scars in his vocal chords. The audience needs to see them through the sound, and they need to hear them through the words. But Zach De La Rocha's voice was only one component I needed.

From the folk side, I borrowed from Jack White, because in my mind, if any other artist could develop what I was trying, it would be him. His voice carried no inhibitions or apologies in his music, and I had never seen anyone generate such force with an acoustic. It was honest yet vulnerable at the same time. A little bit of country and a little bit of rock. This then brought me to Tupac and his acoustic version of *Thug Mansion*. That song was by far the most inspiring acoustic-rap I had ever heard, and I wanted to give that feeling to an audience.

My subject matter would be the deciding factor, and with Bob Dylan in my head, I wanted to write songs that would outlast the radio. This meant avoiding the misogynistic trappings of raps about jewelry, cars, and money. I just wanted to be taken seriously. So by being the only folk-rap artist who could play the guitar and rap, I had a leg on the competition.

I wrote lyrics, beats, and melodies inside my studio; and to capture the voice I was searching for, I got a cannabis card and smoked weed to break my vocal chords in. After the second week of smoking, my roommate Darvin grew some concern and wanted to know if I was okay. "I'm fine," I told him.

"But are you sure?" he asked. "Because I don't think smoking for fourteen days straight is healthy for you."

"Well, if you really think so," I replied, "let's have a race to see how unhealthy I am. I'll smoke an eighth of weed, and you can finish an entire bottle of Ambien, and the one who wakes up first, gets to tell the other to mind his own business and shut the fuck up."

I was in a race with myself, and the only thing that mattered was the music. Of course, I didn't find success right off the bat; in fact, my first batch of songs was a complete failure. But instead of dwelling on it, I plugged away and learned from my mistakes, littering my bedroom with posted quotes on greatness as a motivation. If there is no passion, one said. The greater the loyalty, added another. I quoted Churchill. I quoted Twain. But my favorite quote was from Ray Lewis, who said, "Greatness is by yourself. No one can make you great."

I suffered through years of ridicule from my friends and family, who wondered, if I was really trying to make it in music, why hadn't I come out with a demo? I couldn't explain to them the method of my genius, so I never bothered to reply. My sound took about eight hundred days to develop; and once there, the songs that were locked inside were able to find an avenue.

My first recorded success was inspired by my sister Ramona and the day before I left Stockton for UCLA. I was a high school graduate, and Ramona was a soon-to-be sixth grader; and to celebrate my departure, the neighborhood threw me a going-away party, which was an alcohol-laced night that resembled a Chinese New Year. The food in my parents' living room. The karaoke machine in the garage. The envelopes filled with money. A party stretching into a Sunday midnight that saw me buzzed but not drunk, looking for my sister, who was off with her friends.

"Ramona!" I yelled, as I walked through Fox Creek. "Ramona!" I'd say again, thinking they were playing tag. But she was nowhere to be found, and even though it was late, it was normal for kids to be out on the weekend. I searched for Ramona and knocked on the doors of houses where I might find her. "Is my sister here?" I'd ask, but every house told me to check the other house, and when I reached He-Man's house, it was there where I'd find and lose my sister forever.

He-Man had a little brother named Pivan, who was around the same age as Ramona, and their house was infamous for having royal rumbles among the elementary kids in the neighborhood. And what these rumbles consisted of was what you'd see on television with WWE, which was WWF back then; except in these rumbles, the kids were actually hitting each other. And the reason I knew this was because He-Man and his friends would record these fake-but-real wrestling matches on their video camera and replay them whenever I came over to smoke weed.

"Is Ramona here?" I asked, when the little Asian boy opened the door to He-Man's house. I tilted my head into the duplex, and I could hear the sound of children laughing and yelling. "What's going on?" I asked, but the little boy only smiled. He looked embarrassed and flushed, and as he continued his silence, we stared at each other. "Where's He?" I said. "Where's Pivan?" The boy stepped back and pointed down the hallway. "My sister?" I asked again. "Is she in here?"

I walked inside, past the smell of incense, and stumbled through the living room. The floor was covered in bamboo mats, the kitchen a wreck with plates littered with spicy sauce and rice. "In there?" I pointed, and the little boy smiled, yes.

It's another royal rumble, I thought, but as I stepped closer and pushed the bedroom door open, I found a group of five children staring at the open closet, and just before I was about to ask what was happening, I looked inside the closet and found my sister. Ramona was sitting on a dresser, and beside her were two children having sex. They couldn't have been older than eleven, I thought, and when I turned to see the five children across the room, they continued to watch without hesitation. Pivan was on the bed, his hands wrapped around his tucked legs. The audience was laughing and cheering them on. A half-empty bottle of rum was in the middle of the floor. "Where's He-Man?" I asked Pivan.

"Not home," he replied.

Ramona's face jerked to attention after she heard me, but instead of shame, she smiled and remained seated. "Ramona," I whispered, trying to avoid the sight right next to her. "Ramona."

I remembered He-Man joking once about how his little brother made two second-graders have sex, but I always thought he was lying. The reality surpassed my reality, and for a second, I watched my sister as she stared at the children.

Why was Ramona here, I wondered. Why was she sitting so close? Why was she not bothered? I looked back at Pivan and asked him where he thought He-Man might be.

"My brother go to Jackson," he said. "Went gambling."

The eyes of the five children were faded, and out of disbelief, I looked at the closet again and saw the discomfort in the little girl's face. I heard the panting in the little boy's breath. Then I blinked and whispered for Ramona. "But Dad said I could sleep at Trisha's tonight," she said.

"I'm leaving tomorrow," I told her. "You have to come home now."

Ramona rolled her eyes and jumped off the dresser, walking past me and through the hallway. "I'll tell He-Man you stop by," Pivan said.

When I caught my sister outside of the house, we were standing in the middle of the street, and I grabbed her by the wrist. "What were you doing in there?" I asked, but she bent her arm back and pulled away. "Ramona," I demanded.

My sister adjusted her T-shirt and continued to walk. "Pivan made them have sex," she said. "He bet me that he could make Runi and Chu have sex, but I didn't believe him."

"Did you do anything? Did you touch anyone, or let any of them touch you?"

"Of course not," Ramona said.

I had it in my mind to say something meaningful before I left for UCLA. I was going to give her the key to my bedroom and tell her she no longer had to sleep on the futon in the living room. "It's all yours," I wanted to say. I had made a care package and left it on the bed. The box was filled with bags of potato chips and candy bars, some movies, and a book called *Harry Potter and the Sorcerer's Stone*.

My sister ran ahead of me, and I never uttered the words. She raced back to our house, and eventually she disappeared into the darkness past the streetlight. I could only hear her steps, but even they were dying. She never bothered to call me in my dorm room during that first year in college, and as technology advanced from pagers to cell phones, and from snail mail to e-mail, I continued to lose touch.

Ramona's innocence never stood a chance in Fox Creek's version of morality, and I knew that by the time I graduated from college, she'd be in high school and already well versed in the art of womanhood. The progression came in hints as the years passed by. The bathroom adorned with new scents whenever I returned for the holidays, with the centerpiece being a woman's underwear hanging from the showerhead. A garment too skinny to be considered my mother's. The stories of boyfriends who were older. The dates that never seemed to end.

The opening song on my demo is a recanting of this loss, and its spoken word is coded and rhymed fast, so that I'm the only one who can decipher the translation. My sister meant a lot to me, and even though I spent all those years trying to win her back, I was never around when it really mattered.

When I finished my demo, I saved the files in my computer and called them *Resin Hits*.

<hr />

It was nearing sunset by the time we left McDonald's, and on the drive from Sacramento to Davis, Lefty and Sean argued about generations, while I listened and opened my phone, replaying the list of text messages until I found the 4-1-5 number of my sister. I saved it under Ramona and deleted the disconnected number she had given me; and after staring at the name for a few minutes, I pressed my fingers against the keypad and sent her a message. *"So what brings you back?"* I asked. *"Are you trying to move back to Stockton?"*

We were stuck in traffic, just outside of West Sacramento, and I rubbed the touch screen and waited for her to respond. "So have you ever played baseball or football on the streets, or do ya do all your sports through video games?" asked Lefty of Sean.

"Do you still use VHS to record your movies from HBO," he replied, "or do you use DVR?"

The two of them watched each other through the rearview mirror. "No," said Lefty. "I use DVR, cuz unlike you, I have a social life."

"Oh, yeah," nodded the fat kid. "Well, have you ever been to a Pimps-and-Hos party?"

"What's that?"

The fat kid shook his head and smiled, looking out the window for a laugh. "It's a party where all the guys dress up as pimps and the girls dress up as hookers. Hence the title."

"They really do that?" asked Lefty.

"Yeah, they do. But you wouldn't know that, because you probably go to Bunco parties like my parents and talk about other people and their interesting lives, pretending you're interested in Aunt Jemima's recipe for onion dip." Sean grinned at the rearview mirror. "It's sad being you, isn't it? To have more days in the past than in the future. To have no more dreams. To live vicariously through kids who don't give a shit about you. That high school quarterback you've been following since Pop Warner. The one whose games you attend religiously because you know he's going to the NFL and you want to say you were there from the beginning. Masturbating to all the girls he'll probably screw. The ones you'll never see again in your lifetime, unless of course, you count the strippers you spend your 401K on." Sean bit his lip and turned back to the window. "It must be sad being you. I bet you need a pill to get it up, don't you?"

"That's it, buddy," replied Lefty. He was nodding his head, as if in agreement, his smile and eyebrows inching toward each other. "You jus' gather all that hate up. Let it build inside that chest of yours. An' when it comes time for you to die of that heart attack waitin' in your future, jus' remember that although I've never been to a Pimps-and-Hos party, I do know what it's like to be with a woman." Lefty raised his chin. "Do ya know what that's like? Did ya ever sleep with any of those hos? Did ya?"

The fat kid didn't answer, and when he didn't, Lefty and Z laughed. "You can't brag about the taste if you've never had the honey," said Z.

My phone vibrated, and I read the message from Ramona. "*I'm not moving back to Stockton,*" she said. "*I need you to drive me to Utah. I'm heading to Toronto.*"

"Oh, God," I whispered. I wanted to ask her why, but this was Ramona I was talking to. I guess I should be grateful, I thought. At least we'll reconnect. I had to look at the bright side of things and let her follow her ideas to the end. Every fiber of my being was fighting the urge to be that discouraging voice of reason. "*I can't drive you to Utah,*" I said. "*I'll pick you up in Dublin and take you to Stockton, but you're on your own from there.*"

"*Just make sure you're in Dublin tonight,*" she said. "*And from there, I'll tell you everything.*"

Everything, I asked myself, and made the move to call her, but I didn't. She'd tell the story again when I picked her up, I thought. I might as well keep it to a one-time telling.

The traffic thinned out, and as we entered the causeway that connected Sacramento to Davis, Lefty and Sean continued their conversation. They had made their way to childhood cartoons, with Lefty poking fun at the fact that Sean was raised by Pokémon cards and soccer moms who fought to give children trophies for last place. "But you married these women," replied Sean. "None of this would've happened if you would've been there to read your kids a book. If you would've kept your manhood and not sold it for the sports car that screams douchebag."

"And that's enough," I finally said. "You both have very valid points, in fact, I think the two of you should develop an act together, but I think Z will agree that the two of you should just let it go."

"He started it," said Sean.

"He started it," mocked Lefty.

I pressed the radio button and left the dial on The Eagle, even though it was playing commercials, and raised the volume so neither of them could talk. Then my phone vibrated with a message from Ramona, who said, "*I can't believe you're not surprised to hear from me.*"

"*Why's that?*"

"Well, I mean, after all we've been through, I'm surprised you even answered my text."

"That's funny," I typed. *"Because after all we've been through, I'm surprised you're asking me for a ride. Don't you have other friends who could help you?"*

"When you've done the things I've done," she said, *"and lived the life I've lived, a trusted friend is hard to find."*

"I guess that's what brothers are for."

"Thanks," she said. *"I'm glad you still see it that way."*

I put my phone back in my pocket and Lefty asked me who I was talking to. "Nobody," I said.

We exited Richards Boulevard and turned into downtown Davis, taking a few rounds around the local shops before heading west into campus, where we parked in the student lot beside a row of fraternity and sorority houses. A girl wearing only a pair of cutoff jeans and a bikini top was standing on one of the balconies. She gave us a glance, but then she turned away. "Welcome to college," said Lefty. "I do believe this is the first time I've ever been." He opened the door of the Chevelle and stepped out to stretch. "An' to be honest, I was kind of expectin' more."

The four of us stood on the parking lot and looked at each other. "Now what?" asked the fat kid.

Lefty popped the trunk and said, "That's what," and took a hold of Sean's shirt, pulling him down until he was sitting on the edge of the bumper. "It's too much of a risk with you walkin' around with us," said Lefty. Z reached inside the trunk for the duct tape, and when he found it, he twirled the roll on his finger and waited for Lefty's signal.

"Are you serious?" the kid asked.

"Yeah," nodded Lefty, "but not 'til we find out where Gio is." He withdrew Sean's phone from his pocket and began to thumb through the inbox. "Looks like we've got a few messages from some friends. Nothin' big," he said. "But it doesn't look like Gio bothered to check up on you." He raised his eyes toward Sean. "What kind of friends do you have?" he asked, but Sean said nothing and rolled his eyes.

Lefty paused and I asked him what he was going to write. "You can't let it be too obvious," added Z. "If you ask where he is, he might think something."

The fat kid watched as we postured about our message, and after Lefty typed and erased two texts, the fat kid grabbed his phone and said, "Let me do this." He was calling a number before we could react, and by the time he put the phone to his ear, it was too late to do anything, so we watched. "Hey," he said, and pressed a button to put the conversation on speaker.

"Hey," replied the familiar voice.

"I'm a little freaked out about what happened today, and I don't think I want to stay in Stockton tonight."

"So you want to come out?" laughed the voice.

Sean bit his lip and looked at Z. "Is it cool?" he asked. "I could be there in a couple hours. Can I sleep somewhere or something?"

The voice waited a few seconds. Somewhere in the background, we could hear the sound of people and laughing. "I guess," he said. "There really isn't any room, but we could figure something out. We're staying at the Co-op. I'll text you the address in a second."

"Cool," said Sean.

"But if we ain't here when you get here, we're probably at some house party."

"No problem."

"Cool," said the voice. "I'll see you when you get here."

The fat kid pressed a button on his phone and threw it back at Lefty. "There you go," he said. "Served to you on a platter."

The phone vibrated and it was a message with an address and directions. "So why did you do it?" asked Lefty.

"I don't know."

"But you do know that he'll be lookin' for you after we beat 'im up, don't ya?"

"Yeah, I do."

Sean put his hands out and motioned for Z to tie him up. "That's exactly the problem with your generation," said Lefty. "Things like honor, respect, an' brotherhood are jus' words to you guys, an' you'd rat out your friends before losin' your ass."

"Whatever," said Sean. "You might think you know me, but you don't know anything about me." Z had just finished wrapping the fat kid's wrists, and to scratch an itch, Sean raised his cuffed hands and rubbed his face against his arms. "You know and I know they weren't really my friends," he said. "I might've fooled myself to think they were, but they weren't. They would've invited me if I really was a friend. They only like me because…" He took a breath and slumped his shoulders. "Just tape my ankles, already, and put me in the trunk until you're done."

Lefty sighed and checked to see if anyone was looking, and when the coast was clear, he nodded his head for Z to finish the job. My eyes were pointed down and into the gravel, and I felt sorry for the kid. *Was he an outsider because he was fat*, I asked myself. I couldn't see what was so wrong about him, but maybe, I thought, maybe those guys had their reasons.

Z pulled a final strip of duct tape and hesitated. He didn't know whether or not to cover Sean's mouth again. "Go ahead," said Lefty. "We can't take a chance."

The fat kid tucked himself back into the trunk, but only after looking at all three of us and grinning. He positioned himself and as we shut the trunk, he closed his eyes, as if to fall asleep from the nightmare. "So where exactly is this place?" asked Z. "Is it walking distance from here, or do we have to drive again?"

Lefty withdrew his own phone and searched the directions on Google. "Well," he said, "it looks far enough that we could walk, but given the overall situation of this thing, we should jus' drive." He turned and pointed with his hand south. "It looks like the Co-op is jus' past the overpass." He sniffed his nose. "It wouldn't take more than five minutes to get there. We need to plan this out," he said.

※

It was the scene from *Pulp Fiction*, the one where Jules and Vincent realize they should have shotguns and where they argue about a foot massage.

The three of us sat in the Chevelle. "We're heading into a blind situation," I said. "If we go there with golf clubs, we'll definitely look suspicious."

"No, no. You're right," acknowledged Lefty. "We'll have to jus' use our fists." He released the clip from his Glock and checked his bullets. "If we get pinched by the cops, all of this is goin' to get us a case." He motioned his hands around the car. "We'll park a few blocks away from the Co-op, an' if anythin' goes wrong, the one who can get away'll have to run back to the Chevelle an' drive off." He placed the gun underneath the seat and showed us his key to the car. "I'll leave the key inside the front wheel of the driver's side. So whoever gets here first'll have to dump fat ass an' head back to my house."

"You want us to kill the fat kid?" asked Z.

"No," shook Lefty. "Jus' dump, you know? Drive far enough 'til everythin' is clear, then kick him outta the trunk."

"But how will he get home?"

"I don't care," said Lefty. "That doesn't matter."

"And what about the other two?" I asked. "What happens to the two people that are left behind?"

"They find a way back to my place. Which means doin' whatever it takes."

Z bit his lip and stared at me, and I nodded my head and looked at Lefty. It feels a little overdone, I thought. But Lefty explained that we were looking at some serious time if we were convicted of kidnapping. "If the unexpected happens," he said, "I can't go to prison again. I won't."

I retraced our steps from the beginning of the day, and I thought about the holes in our story, and the fact that if they needed to, the police could find surveillance tape of the Chevelle at Wal-Mart, and the Chevelle at McDonald's. Now would Sean actually report everything to the cops? I didn't think so, but nonetheless, it would be hard to explain anything if we were caught. The prospect of serving time in a federal prison didn't sit well, so I went along with the plan.

Before leaving the parking lot, Lefty searched the Internet with his phone and found Gio's Facebook page, which was under the name George Thiessen, and after I concurred that, indeed, that was the man who had jumped me, Lefty copied and sent the link to Z's phone. "Do ya want me to send it to you, too?" he asked, but I told him I knew the face by memory.

The Co-op was a low-rent housing community for college students, and we spent another ten minutes researching the layout of the complex through Google. "It's at the end of a cul-de-sac," said Lefty. "An' that means there's only one way in, an' one way out." He backed out of the parking space and headed for the apartments. "We'll drive through the area an' get a taste for where we are, an' then we'll park the car in the Safeway lot across the way."

The drive didn't take long, and we were soon idling the Chevelle through the cul-de-sac because of the sudden traffic of people wandering from apartment complex to apartment complex. It was a sea of college students ransacking each other for alcohol and beer; and if the cops hadn't been called yet, I knew they eventually would be, giving us only an hour at the most before the festivities were shut down.

Girls were dressed up and made up and clung together as they searched the streets for friends. It was like New Year's, except there were no old people. It was like Halloween, except for no costumes. Like a dance club that had spilled from a jar. Like a city that had just won the World Series. The boys traveling in their own packs, the majority carrying a red cup in one hand and a blunt or a cigarette in the other. "So this is Picnic Day," said Z. "I think I like it," he said.

We drove and spotted the Co-op, the epicenter for all the partying; and it didn't look like we could start a fight and get away with it. But after all we had done, there was no choice, so we made a U-turn and waded through the current of students and parked the car by the Safeway.

Lefty did like he said he would and put the key inside the front wheel on the driver's side. "Ya think we're a little old for this?" he asked, referring to himself and Z.

"No," I said, but they didn't believe me, so I waited another five minutes for them to check themselves in the side mirror of the Chevelle.

We walked across Richards Boulevard and entered the cul-de-sac, which was growing louder and louder by the second. A group of girls next to us were whooping and hollering about how drunk they were going to get, and in response, you could hear a group of boys yelling at them. "You fucking sluts," someone shouted. "Go suck a dick," another one yelled.

The girls weren't fazed and answered their catcalls with insults about little penises. "Fuck you," added the girl who was wearing a form-fitting black dress. Her eyes were nearly shut from all the drinks she had probably taken. Her arm was resting firmly around the neck of a friend.

I remember college, I thought. I remembered all the nights in Westwood, how we never thought tomorrow would come. And I remembered how I used to carry myself. And as I looked at these kids, I wondered if my face ever looked this young.

⚜

Lefty and Z looked lost, and because I was no stranger to college parties, I took the lead and led them to the backside of the Co-op, where we found a row of five kegs and an endless stack of red cups. It was a crowded line, but eventually, we managed to pour ourselves a drink. From the smell, I could tell it was Bud Light, and after sipping the head from my cup, I told Lefty and Z to pound their first cups because they seemed on edge. It was a lot to take in, especially for them, since they had never attended college. You hear about these parties, and you see them in movies, but when you're actually there, there's no describing it.

My first college party in UCLA was at the Triangle house on Landfair Avenue, which is home to the engineering fraternity. And although I thought most of the kids were nerds, I was surprised at how crazy it got. I snorted my first line of coke off the toilet seat of a second-floor bathroom, and I had sex on the floor with a geology major from Oklahoma. She gave me two minutes before she grew a conscience and ran away.

The Co-op party was full of girls like her; and had things been different, I would've enjoyed myself. "So what now?" asked Z. "Where do we go from here?"

Lefty swallowed some beer, and we followed him away from the kegs and into the grass, near an organic garden that someone from the Co-op was probably growing. "You see these two buildings?" he pointed. "I'll check this one, an' Cali, you check that one."

"And what about me?" asked Z.

"You, my friend, stay close to the parkin' lot an' make sure Gio doesn't leave. An' if either of us finds 'im, go 'head an' send a text."

"But if we're worried about getting pinched," I said, "shouldn't we refrain from sending each other text messages?"

"It's fine," said Lefty. "Jus' text a number an' we'll meet you on that floor. An' if anythin' goes wrong, erase your messages an' stick to the plan." He tipped his cup into his mouth and finished his beer. "First person to reach the Chevelle has to dump the kid, an' the rest of us'll have to find a way back to Stockton. No phone calls or text messages if anythin' goes wrong."

A pop from an uncorked champagne bottle startled us, and we watched as the bubbles were poured onto the shirt of a laughing girl, the smattering of screams and hollers igniting amongst the crowd. "Jus' take your time," said Lefty. "We'll get 'im."

I wiped the beer from my mouth and walked to the building where the kegs were and where the champagne bottle was now being sprayed. The doused girl was still in the spotlight, and as I made my way past her, a wave of red cups were emptied in her direction, which caused a momentary alcohol fight, the red cups being launched like water balloons, the drops of beer being splashed in a cloud of rain.

I opened the door to the first floor to escape the madness and found myself in a hallway covered in the haze of marijuana and cigarette smoke. My fists tightened at the thought that Gio was near, and out of habit my shoulders tensed. I wanted to yell his name, as if we were in a 1980s action movie. The asshole is near, I said to myself. My steps hesitated and I pressed forward through the crowd. Every time I passed an open door, I stuck my head inside and readied myself for a fight, but every time I checked, it was always a false alarm. The strangers in each room would greet me with the same look, and then they'd ask me if I needed something.

Gio wasn't in any of the rooms on the first floor, and he wasn't in the kitchen or in the communal bathroom. I checked my phone to see if Lefty or Z had found him, but there were no messages. "Where is he?" I whispered, and opened the hallway door and proceeded to walk up the stairs.

I looked up and across to the other building and saw Lefty making his way into the third floor. He nodded his head to ask me if I had found him, but I nodded back and said no, and then he responded with a shrug of his shoulders and opened the door to the third floor. I shook my red cup and saw that it was empty, and then I threw it over the stairs. The party was getting louder, and in the distance I heard a police car heading in our direction. I leaned over the stairs to see if anything was happening in the parking lot, but other than the crowd of college kids, there was nothing to worry about. The siren soon faded to the backdrop, and I continued my search and opened the door to the second floor, where, again, I was met with the haze of marijuana. Yet unlike the previous floor, there was something happening, something big.

I could see a group of kids with their camera phones recording an event inside one of the rooms. It was an overflow that had congested the hallway, and each kid was pining toward the door for a better angle. My fists clenched again in reaction, and I prepared myself for the possibility that Gio was somehow involved.

As I walked, I made sure he wasn't in any of the other rooms, and before I could make my way to the noise at the end of the hallway, I turned right and into the bathroom. The floor sticky with a run of mud and urine; I pulled the curtain to one of the showers and found a kid slumped on the floor, the empty rum bottle slipping from his hands. "Are you awake?" I asked, but he wouldn't answer until I had slapped him a few times. "Game over," he muttered, his eyes rolled back into his head. I placed my fingers on his neck and checked the strength of his pulse, and after toying with the idea of helping him into a bed or a couch, someone entered the bathroom and met me in front of the shower.

"Is he dead?" asked the someone.

"No," I replied. "I think he's just dreaming."

He bit his lip and turned the showerhead, letting the water fall onto his friend. "That should keep him semi-awake."

"I guess so," I said.

The someone shook his head and asked me if I wanted to see something crazy. "You won't believe what's happening in that room," he said. "You got to see it for yourself."

"What is it?" I asked. "What's going on?"

"Just trust me. You got to see it for yourself. You wouldn't believe me if I told you."

He tapped me on the shoulder and motioned for me to follow him. I took a last look at the kid in the shower and tip-toed through the path of mud and urine. The yelling was louder now, and there were more phones recording the event. "Come on," he said, as he entered and vanished inside the mob. I used my hands to part the masses and wiggled my way through the bodies until I was able to squeeze through the doorway and into the dorm.

A woman with her head covered in a paper bag meant for groceries was naked on the edge of a bed. Her legs were moist with sweat and they were wrapped around the waist of a man who was fucking her, and they were surrounded by a group of three other men, all of them naked and apparently waiting their turn. She was jerking back and forth with each thrust, and as the intensity rose, so did the chants from the onlookers. It wasn't rape, but it was far too morbid to be anything else.

The woman's legs released the man after he had enough, and without losing rhythm, she stood on the floor and bent herself over the mattress, inviting the courage of the next man. "Fuck-that-shit," they chanted. "Fuck-that-shit!" Over and over again until the next man took his turn and entered. She was entertaining them, and I wondered why and I wondered how.

The paper bag began to inch away from her head, and as her face revealed itself, I saw visions of my high school sweetheart. Of the fantasy girl and her pictures hidden inside my phone. Of Miranda and her mansion in Redondo Beach. Of my days in McDonald's and all the Filipino brides from the mail-order catalog. The lesbians from the Hilton off March Lane, and all the women I had ever known.

If it was them, I could live with myself, but it wasn't them. It was my sister. They were fucking my sister, Ramona. What are you doing, I wanted to yell. Why are you doing this? Ramona and her face embittered in a place between pain and ecstasy; she had no idea I was there beside the door. It wasn't rape, but like I said, it wasn't consensual.

I looked down at the ground and thought about stopping her, and then I looked to see the faces of the men involved. They were young like her, and had they been older, I could've seen myself doing something. To see them with her, it was like staring into a life I never had the chance to change. What Ramona derived from this exhibition, I'll never know. At one point in our lives, we were brother and sister, but that was before I left for college, before I abandoned her.

The scene was nothing I needed to see, so I turned to the doorway and disappeared.

My fascination with the Santa Monica Promenade dates back to my college years at UCLA, and when

I moved back to Los Angeles after being released from the Honor Farm and after all the hours I put into my music, I decided my coming-out party would be there at the Promenade, in the open-air mall with all the other street artists and performers. If it was hardcore rap, I thought, if my goal was to win the approval of the African-American crowd, I would've earned my stripes in the inner-city rap battles held throughout the state. But I wasn't rapping in the original genre. I was more like Bob Dylan and Jack White and had neither the tongue nor interest to pretend I was black. The folk-rap I developed was for the dazed and confused listener; and in that time I put into my music studio, I honed my look by growing my hair into a mix between a Pacific Islander warrior and a pothead from Berkeley, my beard groomed into a scruff that smelled of an alcoholic looking for his next fix.

It wasn't a contrived look like some might think, but it was a departure from that corporate wannabe I tailored myself into. More of a return to who I really was and how I saw myself. I was a musician; and if a musician is worth his salt, then he should be detached, acting as a mirror for those who would listen.

I had nothing but a guitar and a harmonica that hung around my neck. My strings were loaded with the work of twenty songs that felt ready to be heard. I woke up that afternoon and rode the Metro 704 to Santa Monica, and when I got there, I watched the other street performers and how they worked the crowd. The electronic violinist with his speakers and funky mohawk. The girl with the cello, sporting a gothic black dress. The singer selling her CDs; the one with idol dreams in her eyes. It all made me jealous that I didn't pursue my dream sooner. That I wasted all those years in college, working on a piece of paper that I would never use.

"Look at this guy," mocked a German tourist.

I was setting myself up near the AMC Santa Monica 7 theater in hopes that I would attract a sizable audience. My open guitar case sat next to my feet, acting as a bank for any tips I could muster, my optimism in doubt because I had never performed my songs for anyone—this performance was nothing like my piano recitals growing up. Something's at stake, I said to myself. I'm finally putting it all on the line, showing everyone my cards and throwing my chips down. How many people have truly done this, I wondered.

I could remember the pessimistic expressions of my friends when I told them I was moving back to Los Angeles. I could hear the irony in their words when they said they believed in me, their apprehension that I was underestimating how hard it would be. How I could never sell enough copies of my demo, or even develop a new music genre. "Do I dare disturb the universe?" I remembered quoting.

It took five minutes for me to tune my guitar, and when I raised my eyes to see the moviegoers and shoppers minding their own business, I hesitated and thought about turning back. "But if not now, then when?" I whispered. I pulled the aviator sunglasses from my pocket and placed them on the bridge of my nose. The music is the only thing that matters, I told myself. If I couldn't see them, then they couldn't see my eyes. And if they couldn't see my eyes, they wouldn't know how scared I was and how much it meant to me.

My fingers began to strum through the chords and then my lips embraced the harmonica. It was my ode to Dylan and the free spirit of the Sixties. And when it came time for me to spit my first verse, I didn't stall the way other wannabes do—the sidestepping of the song with preamble about what the song was about. That top-forty hip-hop diction. The uh-huhs. The yeahs. The check-it-outs.

I released my strumming hand from the guitar, and without knowing who exactly was in front of me, I extended my middle finger in the air, and as a gesture, told everyone who doubted me to fuck off.

By the end of the first song, I opened my eyes and saw a group of twenty. And by the end of the night, I would earn a larger following and $213 in tips. A couple of pretenders with misspelled business cards offered to be my manager, but I refused. It was then that I realized I was onto something, and in an act of self-preservation, I was determined to hold on to whatever they were after.

⁂

It was hard to believe that Ramona was having sex less than thirty feet away from me. I returned to the dorm bathroom, and after taking another glance at the kid sleeping in the shower, I splashed the sink water in my face and stared at the mirror. "This can't be," I said. "That can't be her. It can't be Ramona. She's in San Francisco," I whispered. "She's meeting me in Dublin."

I pressed the buttons of my phone and sent her a text message. *"Tell me where you really are?"* I typed. *"Why are you lying to me, Ramona? I know you're in Davis."*

I shook my head and wondered if she'd ever respond. Then I stared at the screen and re-read all her messages, and when a new text vibrated into the phone, I closed my eyes and was sickened at the thought that she could respond so quickly, but then I looked at the screen. It was Lefty. *"Four,"* he said. Gio was on the fourth floor.

I took a deep breath and pressed the power button. I didn't have the time to deal with Ramona's excuses and all her problems. I told myself I'd call her when I was done with Gio, and then I tucked my phone in my pocket and walked back to the hallway. The crowd had had enough.

Either that or Ramona had finished. The kids in the hallway were dispersing from the dorm room, and they were laughing and replaying the event on their phones.

I chose the opposite end of the floor and opened the exit door to the stairs. The parking lot had grown thicker with students, and somewhere in the chaos, I could see Z sifting through the crowd, heading toward the fourth floor of the neighboring building. My fists clenched, and as I bit my lip, I looked up at the fourth floor stairwell across the way and saw Lefty waiting. "It's Gio," he mouthed. My hands grabbed the stair rails and I hurried my steps down to the first floor.

A siren from a police car echoed throughout the Co-op, and just as I was about to run up the stairs and meet Lefty, I turned back to the parking lot and saw a caravan of three squad cars, their sirens rotating the red light, creeping slowly to the Co-op. "He's inside room forty-six," said Lefty.

I was out of breath and panting. The fourth stairwell allowed me the vantage point of seeing the entire party. We only had a few minutes before the police would shut everything down. I leaned into the rails and stared at the second floor where I had found my sister. "What're you waitin' for?" asked Lefty. "He's inside, an' he's playing the guitar to some girl." He pulled me by the shirt. "He won't expect it," he continued. "It's now. We've got to do it now."

The door to the second floor opened, and out came my sister, her arm wrapped around the neck of one of the guys inside the room. She looked faded on a combination of weed and alcohol, her pretty face worn by cigarette smoke and beer. Ramona held her cell phone in her free hand and it looked like she was texting. If it was me, it would have to wait until I picked her up in Dublin. "What room did you say?" I asked.

"Forty-six," said Lefty.

"And what about his friends? Was there anyone else with him?"

"Jus' a girl inside the room," he said. Lefty peered over the ledge. "There's a group playin' beer pong in the kitchen. I don't know. They could be his friends."

The cast on my left hand reminded me of why I was there. I squeezed my fist again and thought about the revenge I had been seeking. "Wait for Z," I said. "As soon as he gets here, come in and help me sort out the mess. If it gets too much for me to handle," I added, "I'll scream for your help."

Lefty patted my shoulder and wondered why I wanted to do this alone, and I told him as quickly as I could, that it was a fight I needed to end. In my mind, a gang fight would only escalate into retaliation, but if I showed I had the guts to face him one-on-one, that regardless of the outcome, we would settle the difference and be free to go our separate ways. "I'll give ya no more than five minutes," said Lefty, and led me inside.

By the look of things, I knew I had more like three minutes and change, so I stepped in, and shifted my focus into another speed. The door closed behind me, and with it, so did Lefty and Z—my only backup. I was alone except for the soundtrack that played in my ears, a ringing that resembled the strum of an electric guitar. The waving of a single note—its repeated strum coincided with my heart beat, the energy distorting my perception of time as I stepped forward and read the numbers on each door.

Forty-six was next to the kitchen and the common living space, and out of the corner of my eyes, I could see the punk kid from yesterday, the one whose nose I busted with the trucks of the skateboard. He was standing in the kitchen, playing beer pong with a group of four or five. There was a gauze bandage covering the bridge of his nose, and even though I hadn't looked directly at him, I could sense that he had seen me. It was his turn to throw, but he didn't. His momentary pause gave him away and allowed me the head start I needed.

My fingers gripped the door handle of forty-six, and after taking a last breath, I rushed inside and without any expectation of what I'd find, I spotted Gio on a futon. He was playing the guitar and serenading a girl to what sounded like Eric Clapton. "What the fuck?" was what he was trying to say when he saw me, but I didn't let him finish. As he tried to get up, I met him with a kick. I took a step with my planting foot and heaved my other leg forward and into the base of the guitar, slamming Gio back into the futon and cracking the acoustic.

The sudden impact sucked the air from his chest and I disarmed him of the guitar. "Oh, my God!" yelled the girl. She was snuggling into Gio before I came in, and now she was creeping back against the other side of the futon. Think fast, I told myself. Her screams were enough to alert anyone else who might help the kid, so I cocked back the guitar like a baseball bat and swung for the fences, exploding the base of the guitar into Gio's face, which broke the neck and left the strings as the only thing keeping the acoustic together. His blood shot across the wall and the girl's screams grew louder. "What are you doing?" she yelled.

I turned around and saw the punk kid with the busted nose. He was running inside when I reloaded the guitar and smashed him in a downward stroke, causing his legs to buckle as he slid into the futon. I had less than a second to close the door, so I dropped the guitar and did everything I could to lock myself in.

The rest of them were banging on the other side, but I soon realized they were useless. To my surprise, the door withstood their efforts. I stepped back to see how, and as a precaution, I checked the dorm room for a chair. There were two of them, one by each desk, so I took the closest one and propped it against the door handle. It would be good enough to buy me some time before they could collectively kick down the door.

The girl took her phone out and tried to take a picture.

"Are you fucking kidding me?" I asked, and snatched the phone from her hands.

"Please," she begged as she surrendered the phone. "Please don't hurt me." The girl was pretty except for her prominent nose; and for a second, I thought about throwing the phone into her face, but instead, I threw it across the room and told her to shut the fuck up.

Gio struggled to his senses, reaching for something he could use as a weapon, his slicked-back hair frayed into pointy pieces over his face. "You bastard," he muttered, before I kicked him again, landing the heel of my foot against the back of his head.

"What did you think?" I said, letting my sadistic fantasies take over. "Did you think that you could kick my ass and get away with it?" Gio bent over the futon and tried to stand. Then I pushed him back. "Fuck you," I said, and punched him in the face. "You motherfucker!" I screamed, and punched him again. His eyes were rolling back. "You broke my hand," I said, "and put my life on hold." I searched the room for something sharp and found that the neck of the guitar had broken into a stake-like shape. "For the next six months, I'll never know if I can play music again."

I picked up the neck and stared at the way it had shattered, the strings snapped and pointing in every direction. "So now, whenever you walk," I said, "you'll never know if you can skate again."

His screams, met my screams, which met the girl's screams, and I plunged the neck into his thigh and stabbed him, digging the guitar as deep as I could, leaving it there, planted inside his body, the strings draped around his leg like vines from a vineyard. The air squeezed from his lungs as I punched him until he passed out.

"We're even," I said, and spit a shot of phlegm on his face.

My right hand was covered in blood by the time my sanity returned. The knuckles had busted open and were secreting their own batch of red. I think it's broken, I told myself. The girl with the nose was hysterical and made a move to open the door, but I pushed her into the closet.

The entire charade was over in a matter of seconds, from the time I entered the fourth floor to that moment where I stood over Gio and his friend. I was right, I thought. They weren't as tough as they thought they were. My hands shook, and after admiring the labors of my work, I stared at the girl inside the closet. She had nothing except the fear in her eyes. Then I listened to the pounding of the others at the door. *Do I make a last stand*, I asked myself. It was a beating I didn't wish to see, so I checked the window.

Beneath the third floor and directly above the second was a decorative awning that covered a window and was big enough to help break my fall. "If they can do it on *Jackass*," I whispered, "then why couldn't I?" Those words and the situation were all I needed to motivate myself. I had done some crazy things in college, and I convinced my mind to return to that place—that dark alley where the border of daring and sanity meet at the point of no return.

I slid the window open once I was ready, and pushed the screen and watched as it landed four floors below. The throbbing in my right hand would soon make way for the pain I'd feel later that night; and much like the fight with Gio, I moved without thinking and threw myself out the window, aiming for the awning which I skidded off of, and fell another two floors, where I took my landing in a row of bushes.

The roar from the crowd in the parking lot did nothing to heal the hurt in my back. When I was falling, my hands were reaching for that imaginary rope that could somehow cradle my fall. But I didn't find it.

"Bro?" someone asked. "Are you okay?"

I sniffed and arched my back and exhaled what sounded like a silent fart.

The bro and his friends pulled me from the wreckage and helped me to my feet. It was more confusing than ever. My body ached, and if it wasn't the voices from the crowd, it was the police sirens and the music from the DJ.

They were unaware of what had just happened inside and mistook me for another college kid on furlough. That I had earned my bruises from the fall. That I had cut my hand in the bushes. That I was a mere undergrad vying for legend status. That I was epic and unaccountable for my actions.

"Are you okay?" the bro asked again.

He handed me what was left of his beer and I toasted in their celebration, looking up at the fourth floor window of my escape, where my eyes met the nose girl who was leaning out and cursing me. From her hand gestures, I could tell she would soon open the door, which meant they'd be downstairs soon enough. I needed to move and lose them, so I welcomed the bro's compliments and began to limp away from the Co-op. By now, the night was dark, and the blackness masked my face and blended me anonymous amongst the partygoers.

I remembered Lefty's plan, and hoped I'd be first to the Chevelle. I wanted nothing more of anyone and missed the routine of my life. "I'm too old for this shit," I said, quoting the line from *Lethal Weapon*. In that instant, the college life had grown sour, and as I walked to the Safeway, I dreamt of lounging in a dive bar and slooping over a drink that made no apologies for its bitter taste.

If this was the audience I wagered my music on, then I felt sorry for myself. The wishful thinking. My nostalgia for a time when newspapers were read. Social conscience instilled and not faked. The days when kids played outside and were left to figure the world. Making mistakes that mattered. The world outside the world I had become a part of. My diary and dreams in the open for everyone to see. It didn't make sense. And then I reached under the tire and sat in the Chevelle, waiting through the hush. And then I turned the ignition and pretended to wait for Lefty and Z. They were nowhere near, and that's when I backed out of the parking lot and drove back to the fraternity houses.

"What happened?" Sean asked when I opened the trunk and freed him from the duct tape. "Your hand," he said. "It's bloody."

"Don't worry," I replied. "Most of it isn't mine."

He rolled the duct tape into a ball and threw it back into the trunk. "What about your friends?" he wondered. "And why are we back in this parking lot?"

"Relax," I said. "My friends are none of your concern." I dusted off his shoulder and handed him the pack of Marlboro.

"What's this for?"

"It's a conversation piece."

"A conversation piece?" he asked. "What the hell is a conversation piece?"

"For when you go to the party, dumbass. If you see a girl outside, you approach her and ask if she has a light." The fat kid's face failed to register my words. "An in," I continued.

"You know? Like another way to start a conversation without feeling like a creep."

"But I hate it when girls smoke."

"You're missing the point, Sean. It doesn't matter if you smoke or not. You can pretend to puff away, or you can pretend to change your mind. All that matters is that she's talking to you and you're talking to her." He stood still, the cigarettes frozen in his hand. "And as for girls who smoke," I said, taking the pack and tucking it in his pocket. "Girls who smoke are like quarts of ice cream. They always taste better on a rainy day."

"But I still don't get it," he said.

"What's not to get? Do you not like girls or something?"

"No," he nodded. "I get the girl part, but why are you telling me this?"

I smiled and nudged him away from the Chevelle so I could shut the trunk. "Because this is where we part ways," I said. I pointed to the fraternity house with all the people. "You're going to walk in there and meet someone."

"Just like that?"

"Yeah, buddy, just like that."

"But what about my ride home? I have nowhere else to stay, and I don't have any clothes for tomorrow."

"That's not my problem," I said. "That's your adventure and your job to figure out."

"So you're just going to leave me here?"

"Yes."

"Well, that sucks," he said.

I wiped my hands against my jeans and watched the fraternity house. "I don't know, Sean. That sign looks like it says Tri-Delta. Now, that could be a fraternity—or even better, a sorority. But you'll never know unless you go there and see for yourself."

The fat kid followed my gaze and together, we observed a group of college students stepping in and stepping out of the house, the volume inside rising and dying whenever the door opened. The girls were in their outfits and the boys dressed formally in their casual clothes. "It sounds like a good time," I continued. "And if I were you, I would rather be in there instead of here."

"I guess," he sighed. "But I don't even have my phone."

"Who cares?"

"But what if someone tries to get ahold of me?"

"Don't you remember anything?" I asked. "I mean, it wasn't long ago when you were a kid and you didn't have a cell phone, was it?" I put my arm around his shoulder and walked with him toward the house. "Like those days when you were young and all you had was a house key and ten dollars that needed to be spent. This is just like that, except instead of ten dollars, you've got ten cigarettes that need to be smoked. Now it's up to you," I said. "Are those cigarettes going to be shared with a group of people? Will you end up giving one to a girl? Or will they be accompanied by a cold beer and whispered conversation because of the music in the air?"

Okay, Sean nodded, his steps marching ahead of mine as I released him. He was five feet away when he turned back. "So you did it," he said. "You guys weren't kidding when you said you'd get Gio."

"It's revenge," I replied. "Isn't that what we're all about?"

"I guess," he shrugged. "But if I know Gio like I think I know him, he's like any other white boy from Stockton."

"And what's that?"

"He's crazy," the fat kid said. "And you can bet that he'll be looking for us tomorrow."

"And maybe he will, and maybe he'll try, but you can tell him that he'll never find me."

"How do you know?"

"Because after this weekend," I said, "you'll never find me in Stockton again."

"And how does that mean anything?"

"Because guys like Gio will never leave the valley. Because guys like him will talk about visiting Southern California, but they'll never know where to go. Because even if they did, they would rather be back in Stockton, talking to the same girls, going to the same party." I started back toward the Chevelle, walking backward and turning my hands into a question. "So what if he finds you?" I asked. "Are you going to fight back like a man, or are you going to take your beating like a chump and befriend him the next day, as if nothing ever happened?"

"I really don't know," said Sean. His eyes took me in for a final time. He knew I meant my words, and that he'd never see me again. "I'm sorry," he said. "If I knew any better, I would've tried to stop them."

The fat kid waved good-bye and walked across the street toward the Tri-Delta house, taking a cigarette from his pocket and setting it against his ear. I thought he'd try the line to one of the girls standing in the grass, but instead, he went straight for the door. If I were him, I would've done the same. A pick-up line always sounds better with a beer.

❧

I pressed the power button on my phone and prepared to text Ramona and tell her there was no need to meet in Dublin. If she was in Davis, why waste our time and gas. The issue of confronting her about the scene inside the dorm room was another matter. Could I ask her about it, I didn't know. What is the polite way to inquire about a gang bang? Should I begin with the story of how I was doing, or should I just come out and ask her?

I waited in the Chevelle and waited the ten seconds for my phone to warm up. At any moment, I expected

Ramona's response to my earlier text. How was she going to defend herself? I was praying for a voicemail and a missed call. That way, I'd at least know I was more than just a ride. It was my only consolation to what I had witnessed, but I was willing to take it.

The text message popped into the screen and it said I had three messages from Ramona. I exhaled and read the first message, and immediately my mind raced back to the friend I had been keeping tabs on through the Internet. *"What are you talking about?"* the message said. *"This is not Ramona, and I am not in Davis. It's me,"* the sentence read. *"Jay Warner."*

But that can't be, I thought. Jay Warner is wanted by the FBI. He's hiding somewhere in Europe, or South America. What the hell would he be doing back in California, and why would he want to come back to Stockton? The obvious answer was that he had run out of friends and money, but why me—why did he choose me?

"This is the same number I've always used with you," the next message said. *"Don't tell me you erased my number."*

"Is this Cali Shock?" the last one asked.

I held my finger above the keypad and considered the hole I was digging myself. I would've given anything to be back in Echo Park, buried inside my bedroom, writing music in my studio while my hands mended. Doing anything it took to forget. To move as far from this day. To be back in my dream. Comfortable in my bubble.

Then my phone vibrated. It was a phone call from Miranda's husband.

"Cali," the voice said.

"Hello," I replied. "Is everything okay?"

He hesitated to tell me the news, but I already knew. "Miranda is dead." I put my bloodied hand over my face. "Are you there?" he asked.

"I'm here…Is there anything I can do?"

The receiver adjusted and clicked a few times before he replied. "We increased the dosage on the morphine and moved her bed closer to the window so she could hear the ocean."

"I know that's what she would've wanted," I said.

"And we've set her funeral for this Wednesday." His voice cracked and he cleared his throat with a drink. "We'd be honored, Cali, if for the funeral, you could play that Brazilian song she loved so much."

"Okay," I told him, and looked at my hands, the left one in a cast, and the right one: bruised and battered into a swell. I was lying, but what else was there to say? "I should be back in Los Angeles by the end of this weekend," I continued. "If it's okay with you, I'd like to drive by the house and give you my condolences."

"Of course, Cali, of course. You can come by at any time."

His good-bye was next, and when I hung up the phone, the screen vibrated with a message from the Ramona number that was really Jay Warner. "*Who are you?*" it said. "*Do you know Cali Shock?*"

☙

On our last trip to Oceanside, Miranda tried to convince me that she was well enough to drive, but from the bandana around her head, it was all false hope. I wrapped her in a sleeping blanket and tucked her next to the sand. The sunset landing into the ocean as the tide rose closer and closer to the road. She was comfortable but had a lot on her mind. We said little during the drive from Redondo, and it made me feel like more of a servant than a friend. That what we were doing was habit and not special.

"Are you okay?" I asked.

She nodded politely and said nothing.

It was only midway through my playing that she finally spoke up. "Any day now," she said, "and I won't be strong enough for these moments."

"And how does that make you feel?"

"Dead," she replied. "It makes me feel dead." The words seemed to jump from her tongue in staccato and hang there, on the edge of her lips. "You want to know what death feels like?" she continued. "It feels like nothing but regret, like knowing that I had my chance to roll the universe into a ball, but I was too scared."

"What are you talking about? You've lived a good life and you've seen more of it than most people will in two lifetimes."

"But if I knew this was all I was going to get, I would've made more use of it. I would've dropped out of those expensive private schools and done something that mattered. I would've listened to more music. Gone to more shows. Drink even more drinks. On and on until I filled my belly of this world." She reached into her pocket and handed me a Jolly Rancher, and after I unwrapped it and put it in my mouth, she spoke again. "I'm so close to the end, closer than I've ever been, and yet I still don't know what's on the other side."

I slid my fingers across the strings and rested my arms around the guitar. "You have to earn an ending," I said. "You don't just fall into one." We smiled at each other and watched a wave crash into the sand. "John Irving said that."

"So what do you think it means?" asked Miranda.

"I don't know. Something. Maybe nothing."

But Miranda wouldn't let go. She wanted to know why, of all the quotes that were out there, why quote this one. "It has to mean something to you," she said. "Tell me why you remembered it."

"I guess the way I see it, from watching people these last couple of years, it feels like we're all trying to write that ending, but we don't know how to get there. Or maybe," I said, "it's not that we don't know; it's that we've forgotten." I ran my fingers through the strings and tried to strum a beginning. "The most powerful word in that quote is the word *earn*. And for whatever reason, ever since I moved to Echo Park, I can't get that word out of my ear."

Miranda hugged her sleeping bag and moved closer to me. "If I were strong enough," she said, "I'd show you all the secret beaches around here."

"It's okay. This one is fine."

"My husband will grieve for a year or so, and then he'll remarry a young girl."

"How do you know that?" I asked.

"It's what you guys do best."

I thought of my father and what he looked like when he flew to the Philippines to buy my mother. How he'd stick out with his black jeans and black T-shirts, and how he'd be loved because of his circumstances and not his character. They told me the story of how they met, and whenever they retold it, my parents would try to make it sound cute, like something out of a Meg Ryan movie, but it never hit me that way. "The loser and the prostitute," I'd tell them. It sounded more like vintage porn, if anything; and I always made sure they knew that.

In the short time I had been with Miranda, I envisioned her as the older sister I never had. I found in her that bond I could never get from an immigrant mother, with whom the roadblocks in diction and language diverted the meaning of my words. My mother could only deal with the literal of what I was saying. The idea of tone had to do more with skin color than sound. She never understood my heartache when I broke up with my high school sweetheart and locked myself in my bedroom.

I carried Miranda to the truck, and as we packed the bed, she said that next time we should watch the sunrise instead of the sunset.

"That sounds good," I said.

We both knew that sunrise would be in another life, but she did her best to pretend there was a tomorrow. "Since I've been sick," she said, "I haven't been able to surf."

"I've seen the boards in your garage, but I always thought they were your husband's."

"No, they're mine," Miranda said, smiling. "I've surfed for most of my life. Gone up and down California, from Santa Cruz to San Diego. I've been to most surf breaks and caught a wave. I wish I could've done more."

"Have you ever done Mavericks?" I asked.

"No," she laughed. "There's the kind of surfing I do, and then there's the kind of surfing they do."

"What's the difference?"

"Big wave surfing is for the guy who wants to roll the universe into a ball and throw it back at God."

"And that's not you?" I asked.

Miranda tilted her head and smirked. "Like I said before, I let go of that person a long time ago. I left her out there in the ocean, and she's been trying to swim back ever since." Her eyes turned to the sea and she stretched. "But this sentimental stuff is too much. No more serious talk, Cali. Tell me something funny. Tell me a joke."

"What am I?" I asked. "Am I a comedian? Is making you laugh a part of my job description?"

We walked back and got into the truck, and she refused to leave until I said something interesting. "I won't give you your keys until you talk." I rolled my eyes and asked her what she wanted to know. "Tell me about the first girl you ever fucked."

I paused and asked her if she was serious.

"Oh, yes," she said. "Tell me about this girl. What was it like the first time you had sex with her? Give me the details. What were you thinking?" I coughed a single laugh and stared. "Well?" she asked. "What are you waiting for? The subject has been decided, and it's time for you to talk, so talk."

"But what do you want me to say?" I asked.

"Just start by telling me who."

I was leaning forward and into the steering wheel, and then I leaned back and sighed. "Some girl in high school. She was my high school sweetheart."

"And what was she? White? Black? Mexican?"

"She was Cambodian," I said.

"Oooh," laughed Miranda. "How exotic!"

I put my hand out for the keys, but she held them away from me, swaying them back and forth. "Not yet," she continued. "I want to know how you convinced her. I want to hear the romance." Miranda lowered her hand and pocketed the keys.

"But there wasn't any romance. It was her birthday, and we were young, and we skipped school and did it at her parents' house." I swallowed and sucked my lips in and motioned for the keys, but the little snippet I had given was not enough. Miranda's shoulders shrunk back and she gnawed on the image I had given her. "It wasn't what I expected," I said, "and we tried a couple more times, but I never got the chance to do it well."

"What you expected?" she asked, her face grimacing. "What does that mean?"

"I don't know, Miranda. It was just a lot to handle the first time. I'm not comfortable talking about it, so just give me the keys and we'll go." I put my hand out again, but again, she refused.

175

"There's no such thing as uncomfortable, Cali." She pointed at me and then back at herself. "You know me, and I know you. There are no secrets, and you have no choice. Now tell me what it is you want to say but won't say because you're scared of being impolite."

I closed my eyes and remembered how we snuck into her parents' house. We had only kissed and touched to that point, and that day would be a first for many things. "I expected something smooth and elegant, but it was more like spoiled roast beef."

Miranda reached around my shoulders and caressed my neck. "It really bothers you," she laughed.

"Well, yeah," I replied. "You have to understand that it was the latter part of the 90s, and shaving was yet to be in vogue among high schoolers." My hands came together in an effort to recreate the scene. "We were naked for the first time," I said. "I was excited, and although her body looked good in clothes, she didn't look the same." Miranda's fingers graced the back of my head and I stared into the steering panel as she massaged the story from my lips. "Her breasts were perky in a bra, but there they were, unwrapped and full of stretch marks, the little tiny hairs sticking to her nipples."

"Go on," she smiled. "What else?"

"And then we did the negotiation."

"Which was what?"

"You know," I said. "It was the I'll-go-down-on-you-if-you-go-down-first conversation that killed what was left of the romance, and which I lost, because she knew that if she went first, I would've chickened out and never returned the favor.

Miranda's smile grew wider. "And what was that like?"

"It was horrible," I said. "I choked on her hair, and that smell grew stronger the longer I was down there, which for a long time, I thought was normal. But only after I got into college did I realize this girl had something wrong with her."

"Well, it ain't that pretty from our end, either," she said. "The man's penis looks like the nose of a sad clown, and it smells like a bunch of lies and broken promises."

Miranda laughed again and our eyes met, the awkwardness followed by a bout of silence that neither of us knew how to break except with a kiss. Her lips shot in and wrestled with mine for a second until she pulled away. Her hands retreated to her side of the car. She turned away from me and handed back the keys. "What was that?" I asked.

She snapped her head and looked into my eyes, and then she rested her head on my shoulder. "That was nothing but curiosity." Miranda exhaled and held me. "I love my husband, Cali. But I wanted to know what that felt like. You won't tell him, will you? It was just an innocent kiss."

"Of course," I said, and turned the ignition and dropped the car into gear.

It was our little secret, and it made me remember what it was like to fall in love. She opened my eyes to the memory, and when I came home that night, I went straight to my desk. For hours, I tried to capture that feeling into my guitar, writing lyrics to a riff and beat that I couldn't get out of my head. It sounded in tune, but it didn't fit my voice, it didn't match my experience.

The next morning, I surfed through Facebook and found my high school sweetheart. Her account was blocked except for the pictures. She looked happy with her family, and for a while, I hovered my mouse around the add button. "You wake up one day," I whispered, "and you realize you'd trade the dream for something else."

It's not that men can't forget their first love. It's that they can't forget the idea of their next.

⚜

I read the text from Jay Warner and replied, *"This is Cali Shock, and I'll call you in a few minutes."*

The Chevelle started, and I drove down the road, looking at the Tri-Delta house. Sean was either a man mingling with a beer and conversation, or he was isolated against the wall. It didn't matter to me. The art was something he'd have to figure out on his own, but I said a prayer and wished him the best.

The highway back to Sacramento was empty, and in ten minutes, I was across the causeway and parked at a Denny's in West Sacramento. The waitress offered water and coffee, and I told her I'd take both. Jay Warner wouldn't be in Dublin until after midnight, and the clock on my phone said I had three hours, so I sat in my booth, waiting for the shock.

From my jeans to my shirt, and my face to my hands, I was either in pain, bloody, or both. The family of four sitting across from me couldn't keep from staring. The old man grinned and acknowledged my presence, and after bowing back, I got up and washed the dried blood from my cast and hands.

"It was a car accident," I told the waitress, as I sat back in the booth.

She hadn't asked, but you could tell by the way she poured the coffee that she wanted to know. "That must've been some wreck," she smiled.

"It must've," I replied, and sipped on the cup.

"Well, take all the time you need, honey, and I'll come back when you're ready to order."

The old man grinned again and I tipped my coffee in his direction. "Good evening," I said, but he pretended I hadn't said anything, so I raised my cup even higher. "I said good evening."

"Good evening," the old man replied.

"It was a car accident."

"Excuse me?"

I scratched my head and raised my voice. "I said it was a car accident." Then I stood up. "A car did this to me," I continued. "I thought you might want to know so you wouldn't have to wonder anymore."

My brashness seemed to embarrass all four of them, so I sat on the other side of the booth and browsed through the menu for food. "I'll have the All-American," I told the waitress. "Scramble the eggs and give me one bacon and one sausage." I wasn't hungry, but I wanted something to offset the coffee.

I had three hours, and if I took away the two-hour drive to Dublin, I had about an hour to kill, and for some reason, I wanted to visit my mother at the McDonald's on Kettleman and 99. Of all the people, I felt she deserved to know where her daughter was and what she was doing. And if anything, I'd get Ramona's real number and confront her. That, above all else, was what weighed on me as I sat and ran my fork across the All-American breakfast.

Jay Warner. The hell with him. He was a fugitive and if I was his last resort, then he might as well have called the Feds.

Nonetheless, my curiosity got the best of me again, and I tried calling him twice, but each time the call went straight to voicemail. *"I'll see you in Dublin,"* his text said, and from that point, all my questions would have to wait.

I ordered a refill of my coffee and thought about ditching the whole idea and driving back to Echo Park. My manager hadn't called with any news; and with no updates, I jumped to the conclusion that the record label didn't feel or understand my music; that if it couldn't be danced to at a club, then why bother? The world had a million musicians waiting to exploit themselves, and I wasn't one of them. If they wanted someone hood, or someone they could auto-tune, then I'd go back to piano and play at a jazz club for tips and drinks.

What I saw at the Co-op was enough to convince me that the world no longer hungered for real music, and had decided to feast on a plate of high-calorie beats that was nothing but fast food to the ears. Anything to keep the party going. Anything to keep from thinking. Whatever to make her move. To make her hips swivel. To keep her a whore. That's what the industry played, because that's what the audience wanted.

I topped my coffee with another coffee and remembered the rap battle in Hollywood my manager invited me to. A dimly-lit club and a hundred wannabes who couldn't write a note. The cameras recorded every second of every minute so they could chop the film into episodes they could broadcast on YouTube. I think I stayed for two battles and berated my manager for taking me to such an event. "Either get with the program," I said, "or you're fired."

The more I thought about it, the more I wondered why we were still together. He always said he liked the idea of folk-rap, but the closer we got to signing a deal, the more he'd try to sway me toward something else. "You record it this way," he said, "and we add a beat later so they can play it on the radio."

To become famous as an artist—that scared me, because whatever happened, I realized I'd have no control of either my image or my sound. I had read enough musical history to know this and become paranoid, and as I finished my fourth cup of coffee, I opened my phone and listened to the first YouTube video I posted on the Internet. It had only been a few years, but already I looked nothing like the musician I intended to be. If you compared it with my latest video, you could tell the money had been spent to groom me, to fashion and mold me into this thing whose only purpose was to make money.

I'd be a flash in the pan if I continued on this trajectory, but what power did I have to stop this? Could I really decline an offer if it came this weekend? I surfed aimlessly on my phone to find the answers; and after paying my bill, the solution still eluded me. I wanted to punch the first idiot I saw and knock some sense into him.

I imagined a douchebag with a Facebook account and pictures of himself in a fixed position. A waif who had no idea that he was useless, that the space he took in the world would have been better spent on fertilizer or waste management. The entitled idiot who wakes up after high school and has nothing, absolutely nothing—no job, no car, no woman, not a single prospect or anything to get him out of bed. I wanted to punch him straight in the face and hear that snapping sound of bone against skin. I wanted to watch his reaction as I took the nothing he had. I wanted to squeeze him and listen to his excuses.

I grew manic in that frame of mind and drove the Chevelle out of the parking lot, dropping the accelerator and speeding down the 80, hoping a policeman would stop me and end this night. Then I merged south into the 99 and opened the window. A gust of air blew through me, and eventually I regained control and lifted my foot off the pedal. I was back at the speed limit, and as I drove south, it became clear to me that I needed to call my sister. We were running parallel, and if I didn't stop her now, she'd be thirty with nothing but regret.

"What am I thinking?" I asked. "I'm getting worked up over nothing. I'm going crazy over thoughts. I'm angry, but I don't know who to yell at. I'm being screwed, and I can't turn around and see who's screwing me."

"Fuck you!" I screamed to the wind. "Fuck you," I repeated. From Galt and into Lodi, that's all I said. The Chevelle wove through late-night traffic, and my mouth cashed in on all the jealous feelings I had ever known.

Oh, what I would've given to be the Asian stereotype. To grow up in a strict house. To be belted for bad grades. I would've taken it all if it meant I'd have a family.

"Fuck you!" my words said. It was the only thing to say, and it felt so good to say it.

❦

When I arrived at the McDonald's, the dining room was closed and I didn't see my mother's car in the parking lot. I idled the Chevelle to see who was inside, and then I drove through the drive-thru and ordered a Happy Meal for the hell of it. "Give me a hamburger and Coke," I said, and pulled into the first window.

"Out of five," said the cashier when I handed her the five-dollar bill. My name was on the tip of her tongue as soon as she saw me, and then she smiled. I remembered her for being an airhead and for the time we snuck into the freezer so she could show me her bra while I showed her my stomach. It was a girl I had known from my brief time with McDonald's, but her name had escaped me. "Cali," she said. "What are you doing here?"

"I'm just passing through," I replied.

"Well, your mom isn't here, if that's who you're looking for. She's working the morning shift and won't be here until five."

The name tag said Nikki, so I went with the name tag and told her I had just been up in Sacramento and was on my way back to Los Angeles.

"My God," she replied, ignoring my words. "What happened to you? Your hands? Your face?"

"I got in a car accident. It looks worse than it feels."

Her hands lingered as she gave me the change, and then she told me she was due for a fifteen-minute break. "Meet me around the front," she said. "We can share a smoke and catch up."

That's just what I need, I said to myself. Waste another fifteen on a conversation I'd forget in five. What else could she tell me that I didn't already know? She was a crew member when I worked there, and since she didn't have a crew leader or manager shirt, it was obvious she had been making minimum wage for the last ten years. But the funny thing about a woman? She could've been the fry girl for all I cared. If she said yes, I would've slept with her, and so would a hundred other guys.

Nikki opened the side door and met me on the sidewalk near the garbage dump. "It's cold," she said, zipping her jacket and taking a lighter and a pack of Parliament Lights from her pocket. "Is that your car? It's pretty sick."

"Uh, yeah," I lied, as she handed me a cigarette.

We puffed for a few seconds and let the nicotine run its course through our lungs. Then we smiled at each other and talked. "So what have you been up to?" I asked. "I haven't seen you since forever."

"I know, right? You just kind of up and left after high school. I bet you're some lawyer or something now." Nikki spoke with a ghetto-valley twang that bordered on country, and the way she was nodding with every word, I half-expected her lips to fall off as she spoke.

"Not exactly," I replied. "I graduated from UCLA and dabbled in real estate for a minute, but now I'm just living in LA."

"That's cool," she said. "So what are you doing now?"

"I'm a musician. I'm doing the LA thing. Trying to make it in the music business." The words sounded horrible, but I wanted to tell her how I'd gained a following on the Internet. I wanted to tell her I had a manager. I wanted to show her that I'd performed in shows and been doing well. But for some reason, I was embarrassed to say any of it, like I didn't believe in myself. That I knew I was failure.

"Oh, right. Your mom said you were trying to be a rapper."

"Yeah," I said.

It sounded even worse coming from her mouth. Who did I think I was, Biggie Smalls? To explain my plan to her—she'd never understand my version of hip-hop.

"So rap for me," she said. "Spit a few verses and let me hear your stuff. I've got a friend who battle-raps in Stockton, and he's pretty good."

Oh, great, I thought. The girl was annoying me, and now I was being lumped with all the other posers.

Nikki finished her cigarette and stomped the butt on the sidewalk, taking and lighting another as she waited for my rap. "I'm cool," I declined, and asked her for another cigarette.

She passed the lighter and a stick, and then I turned the subject to her. "So what about you?" I asked. "What have you been doing?"

"I'm a mother now," she replied. "I got married and now I've got two daughters, Destiny and Alizé. You didn't know?"

"No, I didn't."

"Well, you probably know my husband. You guys went to the same high school."

"Oh, really?" I asked. My hands fiddled with the lighter and my mind ran through the list of friends.

"It's Jose. You remember Jose, don't you? Jose España?"

The name didn't ring a single bell, but I nodded and said, "Yeah, I remember Jose."

If Nikki was a guy, I'd punch her for naming her daughters after a stripper and a drink. It's true, she really didn't say much to deserve it, but as I stood and shared a cigarette with her, I grew disgusted. She did nothing with her life and had two kids to show for it. And me, I thought. I graduated from college, and had nothing except a dream. The comparison felt bitter, and I began to play with the lighter, clicking it on and off as she continued to describe her little family.

They had a rented house, she said, and she described the problems that came from renting, each of them major, all of them important. The twists that required fixing. Then the dental appointments for the girls, and so on and so forth until she received a phone call. "It's my Dad," she said, and pressed the button to speak. "Hello?"

Nikki turned away from me, and because I felt like doing it, I followed her steps and lit the lighter against the locks behind her head, touching the flame with her split ends and watching as it quickly caught fire. In ten seconds, she'd be bald. The flame grew bright, and then I grew a conscience and patted her on the back, snuffing the fire into a smoke. "I got to go," I said. "Thanks for the cigarette."

The girl had no idea and gave me a hug. "I'll see you soon," she replied, and I handed her the lighter and returned to the Chevelle.

I stopped at the Chevron on the other side of 99 and Kettleman and filled the tank with forty dollars' worth of gas. A bum approached me for change, and I gave him the Happy Meal instead. From his sunken eyes, food was the last thing he was hoping for. The man dipped his hand into the bag and watched as I drove away.

A kid in a Honda Hatchback tried to race me from the 99 into the cross-town, but from the sound of his engine, the kid switched his stock for a Toyota Supra, so I gave him the thumbs up and let him speed ahead. Besides, I thought, it wasn't my car to begin with. The last thing I needed was Lefty with a grudge.

I took the 5 into Weston Ranch and parked the Chevelle in Lefty's driveway. Neither Lefty nor Z was around, so I put the keys underneath the wheel and sat in my truck, waiting for the engine to warm. It'd be another thirty or forty minutes to Dublin, and at that point, I was running low on energy and didn't feel like talking to anyone. Miranda is dead, I said to myself. The image bothered me, and I couldn't let go.

She'd be buried and returned to the earth on Wednesday, and where would that leave me? She was the only woman I respected, the only woman who understood what I wanted in life and who I wanted to be. I can't, I thought. The woman prepared me for her death, and on numerous occasions, I assured her that I'd be happy when it happened, but as it was, I could do nothing but sit in my truck and think.

The tears welled from inside of my stomach and eventually, they began to run from my eyes, pouring over my cheeks and onto my shirt. My chest convulsing to keep it together, I hunched over the steering wheel and lost control. "Why?" I whispered. "Why does it end this way? What did she do? Why? Why? Why?"

I folded my hands over my face and pressed my thumbs underneath my chin, breathing in through my nostrils and out through my mouth. The caffeine on my breath smelled raw, and it had me thinking rapidly as I tried pinching my temple to slow it down. At any minute, I expected my brain to hemorrhage with a tumor of incoherent words and notes. A cough of acid reflux that tasted like bad orange juice. The blood that would drip from my ears. That ringing sound from an overcharged amplifier.

"Finish this day," I said. "Just do what you have to and finish this day."

I dug my nails into my scalp and turned the radio to KNBR 680 and listened to a caller talk about the Giants and their pitching rotation. "If Tim Lincecum can smoke a few bowls," he said, "I think he'll retire as a Hall of Famer." The discussion brought me back with a laugh and reminded me of childhood baseball games and days when you didn't need permission slips to play with friends. Then I opened the window to freshen the air and left Weston Ranch for the 5 and Jay Warner.

My truck's windshield was covered with the dead bodies of mosquitoes and gnats, and since my gas tank was running low, I headed west on the 205 and exited Tracy Boulevard to fill my tank at an ampm. The handheld windshield wiper seemed dull, but I dipped it in the water and scrubbed the dead bodies off the glass. The crunching sound of the wings getting crumpled vibrated into the handle, and after putting the wiper away, a black man with cornrows approached me and asked if I was looking for anything. "You want trees?" he said, speaking in code. "I got trees, rocks, even bitches. You name it, brah."

He said his name was Denzel, and I lied and told him I didn't do drugs anymore but that I admired his hustle nonetheless. "You listen to music at all?" I asked, and reached into my truck for a CD. "It's a little bit of rap, a little bit of folk. You might like it if you give it a shot."

"This you?" he replied, staring at the case. He flipped it over a few times and smiled. I could tell the title on the CD had gotten his attention.

"I recorded it in my homemade studio," I said. "It took me forever to get it the way I wanted, and I must've smoked a pound of weed if not more. And that's why I called it *Resin Hits*."

The left side of Denzel's face smiled and he bobbed his head to feel my story. "I like it," he said. "I like it."

"Then go ahead and take it," I replied. "You can have it for free."

"Nah man, it's cool," he said.

"I'm serious. Go ahead."

He wavered for a second. "You sure, brah?"

"I'm sure," I said.

The CD didn't cost much, but I figured if he listened to it and liked it, then maybe his other drug friends might pick it up, and then from there, the word could spread. I'm a folk-rapper, I thought. I should just take control of my career and go back to doing it the way I want to.

I gave Denzel a handshake and a shoulder bump, and when I returned to my truck, I took my phone out and made a move to erase my Facebook and YouTube account, but then I remembered my manager and came to my senses. It'd be disrespectful to destroy our hard work without discussing it first. The dreamer in me wanted to hit the road and play in small venues that catered to the lowest denominator. That's the cut of my skin, I thought. Why am I pretending to be something else?

※

From the 205, my truck climbed through the Altamont. The moon illuminated the backdrop of hills, and in the distance, I could see the windmills scattered across like white freckles. If there really *was* an energy crisis, I thought, the real music would survive and the rest would fade in an afterthought. Then maybe, just maybe we could slow dance again. "I know I'm crazy," I said, "but I can't remember the last time I did it."

The downward slide into Livermore glided the truck, and my speedometer began to scale toward the right and into the 90s as the 205 merged into the 580. I was less than twenty miles from the Bart Station, and when I saw a police officer parked off the highway, I stepped gently on the brake and made a move into the slow lane. With my budget, I couldn't afford a ticket; and as I passed the officer, I checked my rearview mirror to see if he would follow.

The road was cracked with the occasional pothole, but my truck made out fine. After driving for another ten minutes, I took the Hacienda/Dublin exit and turned left on Hacienda, then right onto Owens Drive, parking my car in the lot beside the parking garage. My clock said 12:36 a.m., but I didn't see Jay Warner, which made me wonder if this was really a joke.

"*I'm here,*" my text said. "*My truck is next to the ticket booth before you enter the breezeway.*"

I pulled the handle next to my chair and reclined into a comfortable position. If the FBI or anyone else had been intercepting our messages, I didn't care. The parking lot was half-full, and there could've been agents hiding in the wake, but I knew I had done nothing.

※

My phone vibrated, but it was Kelly, the fantasy girl from the hotel. *"What are you doing?"* she asked. *"By any chance, are you still in town?"*

"I'm in Echo Park," I lied. *"I'm on my way to a party."*

The girl said she was lonely and sent a series of messages about what she had done today, but by the sixth text, she had grown horny and wanted to flirt. *"Call me,"* she said, *"and let's play."*

"I can't," I replied. *"I'm on the road."*

"Just park your car and let me listen to the sound of your voice."

We argued over a few messages and then she sent me a picture of herself lying naked in bed.

"It looks good, Kelly, but I'm really busy."

The woman was used to having her way, so she responded with a video that began with her licking her hands. *"I'm all wet,"* she said. *"Send me another picture and I'll let you go."*

I turned and checked the view from every window and saw no one. It wasn't the first time I had done something like this in a parking lot, but this is what it's like, I thought.

This is normalcy, and if I wanted to live in this world, I would have to get used to it and pull my zipper down and send her a picture.

"*Make it hard*," she replied.

It was never enough for this woman.

With the cast on my left hand and the swelling and bruises on my right, I LOL'd her and told her I had reached my destination and would call her back. "*See ya*," I said, and sat in my truck, replaying the eight-second video she had sent me.

※

I was bored and in need of a drink, and as I waited, I listened to *Home* by Kanye West and broke apart the rhyme scheme and beat. The chorus resonated with me, and I tapped my thigh to imagine the monologue Kanye went through as he wrote the words. "Go ahead roll it up and pass it round," I sang. "Cause lately's been a whole lot of bullshit going down. A lot of soldiers ain't make it through this year, so let's just celebrate that we still here and whoa." The beat galloped at a horse's pace and I arched my back and pushed my chest every time the bass dropped. "Never leave me alone," I continued. "Tell 'em holla at ya boy cause I'll be coming home. I'll be coming home."

I transposed the rhyme scheme and imagined how I could incorporate the rhythm into a song led by an acoustic or electric guitar. Then by sheer luck, I remembered a violin cover of *Mr. Brightside*, and with my phone, I logged into YouTube and listened to the sound and took notes and composed a draft of a verse, using my notebook to record the lyric that summed up the night. Of revenge. The prodigal son's return. Of family and its impossibility. That unmistaken way a woman can look at you. Of dark nights and dive bars. Of friendly conversation that seems to mean more than it is.

My busted hands simulated the notes from a piano as I continued the tapping on my legs. I heard the music even in silence. I heard the words in my head. It wasn't perfect, but the revision could wait. The piano took off and receded into my subconscious, and every note took me to a place farther and farther away from here, wherever that was, whatever that meant. And then I added the ensemble of the violin and imagined the song as a duet. That long yearn against a bow of horse hair, resin, and maple wood.

I fell in love with the gallop; and if I could've, I would've drunk a case of beer and lived on that gallop for as far as it could've taken me. "Badaba, badaba," I whispered. "Then I sing. Then I wow. Then I who. Then I sing. Then I wow. Cause I can. And I will. If I could. Bring the bill. Cause I am. Cause I'm now."

It was a framework at best, but I couldn't stop. Baba. Dada. Baba. Dada. It was incessant, and as I began to sweat, I was disappointed when the YouTube cover ended, so I pressed the play button and restarted the sprint, my head tilting from side to side. Its recapture liberated me again, and all at once, I was strumming the guitar, stringing a violin, and pounding on a piano for perfect octaves that would come as they needed to, in phrases of three, in places I vanished to when I was lost, that savior, that escape.

And then I was haunted by the past; and when I looked, I knew it was Jay Warner knocking on my door, and in the midst of this jubilation, I had my options and decided on the latter. He had nothing but the clothes on his back. Jay Warner opened the door and sat beside me.

❧

"What are you doing?" he asked, as if time had never done its job to separate us. "You high or something?"

We slapped hands into an arm wrestling grip and gave each other an embrace. He was a convict, I told myself. I expected the unexpected. A whole brigade of agents that might descend upon us, or a single shot from a sniper who had been swindled, but neither occurred, and Jay Warner looked nothing like Jay Warner. His skin was tanned in symmetrical tones. He had lost so much weight that he bordered on sickly. He had either done work on his eyes, or he had gotten into marathon shape. It was a time machine, and if he played the right words, I would've driven him to Cape Froward, if for anything, so I could hear the misadventures of his hide-and-seek from the law.

"Hurry up. Hurry up," he said. "I don't know if they're wired into my phone, but let's not wait to find out."

I started the engine, and before we entered the highway, he asked me how much I'd take for my truck. "Name a price," he said, "and it's done."

Jay Warner wore an apathetic smile. It had done little since the last time we talked, and there were no signs of remorse or regret. "Don't say a number," he continued. "Just call it like you need it. One stack. Two stacks. Even three. Just let me know."

He admitted that he knew his schemes would end this way, but what did it matter if it meant he could get so much money. "But you look broke," I replied. "What good is the money if you're always on the run?"

"But you're wrong, Cali. I might have no money in my pocket, but I'm everywhere."

The reunion played like nothing I thought it would. We were doing little in terms of reacquainting ourselves, because in Jay's eyes, it was 2005 and we were still in our prime.

He explained that the phone number he had been using with me and a few others was under a fake name that could never be traced back to his real identity. "Some James Bond shit," he laughed.

Jay kicked his feet forward and leaned back, peering into the darkness, at all the sights he had known in a previous life. "I lost them in Tel Aviv," he said. "They were hot on my trail, but I flew to China, and from China to Indo, and from Indo to Japan, Vancouver, and San Francisco."

"There's something waiting for me back in Stockton," he continued. "Go to the Extended Stay hotel on March Lane. The one behind Dave Wong's."

We were driving fast and talking faster, and it wasn't until we reached the 2-0-9 that it slowed down into real time. My truck taking the March Lane exit like he said, I turned left and into the parking lot. We were caught in the middle of the Chinese restaurant and the adjacent hotel, and when I killed the engine, it was silent. The two of us waited, and I raised an eyebrow, measuring his next move.

"Wait a second," I said, grabbing his hand as he moved to open the door. "I haven't seen you in years, and you act like it's normal, like you're not wanted and this is another day at the office."

"You sound like a girlfriend," he laughed. "It's just me. There's no reason to reflect on my return. In fact, there isn't much time."

"What does that mean? You're not making sense."

"I'm moving at a hundred, and I've been doing so since customs in Vancouver. And you're sitting there moving at fifty, trying to catch up to something that won't happen." He turned a hand over and shrugged his shoulders. "Either pick up the pace, or get left behind."

Jay Warner opened the door and walked toward the Extended Stay.

I locked my truck and followed Jay to the front entrance of the hotel. The first set of doors was unlocked, but the doors into the lobby were shut. Jay Warner put his hands against the glass and spied into the front desk, which was closed. "We need a key," I said.

"Shhh, shhh, I know. I'm just checking to see if anyone's working." Jay Warner bent down to his shoes and pulled a key card from his sock. "You see, if this were normal, I'd have time to ask you about that cast and those bruises on your hands and face." He placed the card into the key reader and opened the doors as they clicked. "But we don't have the time," he whispered. "It'll be an even longer night if it's not here." It was almost three in the morning, and I was beginning to wonder if I'd ever get to bed.

We entered the lobby, and I watched Jay as he checked the hallway. It was empty, and after pausing to listen for footsteps, we continued into the stairwell and took an exit onto the second floor. You're being paranoid, I thought.

But if I were him, I would've been acting the same way. If I wanted to know how the road had been treating him, I would've found my answer in his face. In the gloom of the ceiling lights, I could see what the darkness had covered so well. Whether it was the stress of the road, or the result of cigarette smoke, Jay Warner appeared middle-aged and fragile, on an eternal bender that would never end unless he was caught.

He's slipping, I said to myself. The man was agitated and walking with extra energy. *If it's meth,* I thought, *he won't last very long.* It could've been an assortment of uppers, but I didn't have the heart to ask.

His lead took us to the front of room 232. "I hope there's no one in here," he whispered, and pressed his ear to the door. "It's a fifty-fifty shot, right?"

"Whatever you say," I replied, "it's your deal."

Jay unscrewed the eyehole from its socket and took his phone out, pressing the flashlight button and pointing it into the darkness inside. "It looks vacant," he said, and inserted the key to open the door.

When we entered the room, Jay turned the lights on and I went straight for the bed, closing my eyes and basking in the relief it gave my shoulders. "No, no, no," he said. "You're going to miss the best part."

I sighed and sat up to see what he was doing. "Before the market crashed," he said, "I took my money and hid it in places I could trust." "You don't remember this place, do you?" he asked, lifting the dresser and moving it forward.

"No, I don't."

"Well, maybe it was you or somebody else, but I used to party in this hotel whenever I came to visit the Stockton branch."

"You never took me here," I said. "We would always go to the Hilton."

Jay traced his fingers across the lining of the carpet, and when he hit the corner of the room, Jay tugged and ripped the carpet from the floor. "I saw this in a movie once. Did you ever see *Stakeout*? It's like that scene where Aidan Quinn returns home to find Richard Dreyfuss sleeping with Madeleine Stowe." Jay Warner knocked on the floorboards and popped a section free. "Now, I thought about doing like the movie and dumping some stacks into the couch over there, but half the time, these kind of hotels are used for prostitutes from Craigslist, and you never know if some kind of accident might happen and they need to switch couches." His hands reached into the gap, and when he found what he was looking for, Jay pulled a gym bag out of the hole and threw it onto the bed. "Go ahead, open it," he said.

I wiped my eyes of the sleepiness and cleared my throat. The bag was heavy and we both knew what was inside. "It's money," I said, unfazed by the find. "I've seen you flaunt gold. I've been to your house, and I've seen the cars and the paintings." I threw the bag back. "So what now?"

"What now?" he replied, unzipping the bag. "Now we negotiate."

Jay arranged the two desk chairs around the first table by the kitchen and sat me down. "I've got more money waiting for me, but I need a car."

"You mean you need my truck," I said.

"That's right," said Jay, "and since I consider you a friend, I'm going to make you an offer you can't refuse."

"But it's under my name," I protested. "If you get caught with my truck, then I'm implicated and it's back to prison; only this time it ain't Mickey Mouse, it's fuck-me-in-the-ass prison, and who knows for how long."

He stared at me and played with the stubble on his chin. "How about that?" he asked, flicking a stack on the table.

"I can't," I said. "Let's just use the money to buy a used car in the morning."

"I need it now," he replied, and threw four more. "All you need to do is this, and you'll never see me again."

"Believe me, that's what I thought when I heard they arrested you, and that's what I thought when I heard you escaped."

"And you had the balls to erase my number," Jay said. "I thought we were friends."

I shrugged and put my hands out. "How was I to know you'd come back from the dead? Besides, I can't take that money. It goes against everything I believe in."

"You sure didn't have a problem when you were working for me," Jay smiled.

"It's different now," I told him. "I feel guilty for all the money I helped you steal. You screwed over a lot of people, Jay. That kind of shit isn't easy to swallow."

He blinked his eyes and began to fidget his legs, his eyes tweaking back and forth across the room. "Look, Cali. I can't begin to describe the lengths it took for me to get here in this hotel. There are places I need to go to, and there are people I need to see. We're talking about things that don't concern you." He dipped his head forward. "Now if you insist on acting like this, you're going to be dragged into something I'd rather not show you." Jay Warner angled his lips. "For your own safety, I suggest you take my generous offer and not fight me on this."

I put my hands on the money and watched as he avoided my eyes. "So what do you want me to do?" I asked. "You want me to report it stolen?"

"Give me two days to get where I'm going, and then you can call it."

I took a breath and agreed to the deal, telling myself that I'd give the money to Ramona when I saw her. It had shady written all over it, but that was the way it was with Jay

Warner. A straight-up trade meant more work and a smaller return.

I unhooked the truck key from my key ring, and handed it to Jay. Then we rolled the carpet back and returned the dresser to its place, and by the time we left the hotel, it was nearly four in the morning. At any second, my mother would wake up and get ready for work. I could've gone back to Fox Creek, but I had no desire to see my father. "Can you at least drop me off?" I asked.

Jay Warner nodded yes.

The sky brightened into a hue of light blue, and as he drove north on the 5, I pulled out my phone and logged onto the Internet, buying a bus ticket through Greyhound, a one-way back to LA. "It's good seeing you," Jay said. "I wouldn't have called, but you were the one I trusted the most."

"It's fine," I sighed. "You know I have your back."

We took the Kettleman exit and headed east toward the 99, and from the corner of my eye, I could see Jay Warner staring at my face. "So now that we have some time, why don't you tell me what happened?"

I slid my tongue around the edges of my teeth. "I got jumped by some skateboarders, and I drove to Davis and settled it."

When he dropped me off at the McDonald's, I grabbed my guitar and my bag. "I guess this is it," he said.

"I guess so."

I reached into the truck and we shook hands. "Good luck," Jay said.

"You too," I replied.

The truck window raised shut, and Jay Warner turned onto Kettleman Lane, but I turned around and averted my eyes to his final direction. *It's better that way,* I thought. Reunions and departures all feel the same. Quick. Lonely. Forgiving.

I sat on the grass by the drive-thru, and tuned my guitar. There was no way I could play with broken hands, so I started to tap the notes on my legs, playing the Brazilian song at first, but after a few chords, I transitioned into AA Bondy and began to sing:

> *And I'm going to leave this town.*
> *With the people all tumbling down.*
> *And my boots on the diamond road.*
> *Behind such a heavy load.*
> *And I will come back someday.*
> *If I do not lose my way.*
> *Don't weep my girl so true.*
> *Let the train whistle cry for you.*

When the world is quiet, I hear an acoustic guitar and all the voices I wish the world would be.

My mother pulled into the parking lot and my phone rang. It was my manager. "They want to sign you," he said, "but…